❧ *Body Parts* ☙

<u>Fiction Series</u>
The Alex Evercrest Series
The River Front
The Girl on The Grill
Missing
Maggot
Racist
Votive Candles
Windy City
Country Road
Pool of Blood
Sins of the Daughter
Body Parts
The Skull Collector
The Vanishing
The Shadow Fighter
Moonshine
Grief's Trajectory
The Magic Touch
Northern Lights
Alex Evercrest Heroine
Alex Evercrest Collection Two
New Direction
Disruption
A Family Affair
The St. Lebuinnus Church Murder

A Brian O'Neil Novel
Hawaiian Phoenix
Moon Curser
Death Broker

The Problem Solver Series
Solutions
Drug Lords
Border Crosser
The Problem Solver Collection

<u>The Taelo Series</u>
Taelo: The Early Years
Taelo: The Golden Feather
Taelo: Journey of Discovery
Taelo: Dangerous Passage
Taelo: Condor Clan Slingers
Taelo: Circumvention
Taelo: The Journey of Sages
Taelo: Collection
Taelo: Future Leaders Journey

<u>A Taelo Story:</u>
White Swan and Quiet Pheasant
The Child's Name
Floating Cloud
Quiet Rabbit
Busy Bee
Little Otter & Talking Wren
Broken Spear
Burley Bear & Meadow Flower
Taelo Story Collection

<u>Science Fiction</u>

The Savitar Series:
Journey's End
Savitar
Confluence
Savitar Series Collection

Bram Nielson Series
The Fold
The Message
Fold Wormhole
Negative Fold
Ripples in Time
Bram Nielson Collection

<u>Single Science Fiction Books:</u>
Current Past and Future
The Event
The Door
Viajante 7

❧ *Body Parts* ☙
By: *Ron Mueller*

Around the World Publishing LLC
Cincinnati, Ohio

This story is a work of fiction. Names, characters, places, and incidents either are products of the author's imagination or are used fictitiously. Any resemblance to actual events or locales or persons, living or dead, is entirely coincidental.

Body Parts ©

ISBN 13: 978-1-68223-996-4

Distributed by Ingram
Cover Picture by: Master 1305 @ShutterStock
Cover Design by: Ron Mueller

Body Parts

1 Business Success

Reston stood in front of the almost live sized human poster of a man with his hands out to its sides. He was surrounded by similar posters of both genders. He was learning the details of the new human body parts business he had been instructed to establish by his bosses in Italy. The poster graphics were detailed and captioned for both the exterior and internal body parts. He felt like a medical student. He was not going to do any memorization, but he knew he would be referring to the posters as the body parts orders came in.

He was use to trafficking in a wide variety of drugs and had never imagined that he would be getting into the business of trafficking in human body parts.

The posters had what each body part was worth.

The arrow pointing to the skin indicated that it was worth thirty thousand dollars.

The scalp was worth one thousand dollars.

He walked around the room, and it became clear that one body was worth more than a half a million dollars if all the parts could be sold.

He wondered about the people that were willing to pay for the body parts. He knew that he would be making more than the half a million per body. The black market return would be many times more.

He had been informed that the legitimate body parts market was a billion-dollar industry. He figured that the black market would be worth to one hundred times more if properly managed

Adding the body parts business to the distribution of drugs had been a path that Reston had not envisioned getting into. He was surprised to find that the company had selected Cincinnati to be the central point of both production, acquisition, and distribution. Many of the body parts were stolen from various legal body parts distributors. The rest would be collected from the appropriate local people.

The posters covered eyes, liver, heart, pancreas, stomach, a large and small intestines, penises, the list went on to cover almost every organ in the body.

He had spent a great deal of time in setting up his own body part production operation. He knew that many of the bodies that he would be asked for would need to be harvested from individuals that he would need to identify.

They that had to be the right match to some person willing to put up the money to obtain the body part they needed. He knew that speed and maintaining a supply of the most desired parts would be important.

He had spent a fair amount of time designing the layout of his parts production, inventory holding room, and distribution supply chain.

His "factory" was located in a warehouse that had all the legal licensing and had passed the required warehouse inspections so that he had a five-year window before the next inspection. He of course had set it up as a regular warehouse and later added the special features that turned it into a human parts production center.

The interior construction had been done by a special group out of the New York area that were all partners of the mafia. They had come in and used the drawings he and a new York architect had made. The work was quickly done in a quiet low-key way.

His few permanent employees were trusted mafia members who had been recruited, trained, and then sent to him.

Recruiting the right person to do the dissecting of the bodies was not as difficult as he had expected. He had forged papers that he presented to the surgeon that he recruited. This surgeon had been on a list of a dozen potentials that had been identified from their participation in a conference on human body parts.

The surgeon was a resident at one of the local hospitals and deep in debt.

He activated his various connections in all the major cities along the East Coast and soon he had a list asking for almost every human body part.

The body parts business was significantly more lucrative than the drug business and distribution was relatively easy since the drug business had an established distribution network.

He kept an eye on the books and soon realized that the money being taken in warranted an expansion.

He was always short of some organ or another. He looked at the back orders and knew that he would need to enlist another surgeon to harvest more parts.

He would also need to be more aggressive in getting the right "donors' on the dissection table.

He had his acquisition leader get more referring doctors enlisted. He was ready to throw the net more broadly so that he could fulfill the surging parts requests.

He spent many an hour watching the harvesting process through an observation window. He had designed a business office that had a window that allowed him to see the dissection table.

He also participated in the inventory inspections of the parts stored in the cold room. Many of the body parts could be held for days and still be used by someone needing it and willing to pay to get around the various waiting lists that prevented them from getting the parts legally.

Those parts that aged beyond their viable period were processed and disposed of in a furnace that operated only at night.

He was making a small fortune running the business.

His surgeon was making one as well.

Reston had set up an offshore account for this surgeon but kept himself on record as a co-account owner. This ensured that the doctor could be kept in check if the working relationship went south. He also tracked much of the doctor's personal life and contacts. He did not want the good doctor to stray from the agreement that had him spending about two hours a day harvesting body parts.

He was currently watching one of the harvesting sessions being performed on specifically ordered body. The good doctor had already removed the eyes. This was an organ that was always in demand somewhere in the country. He was currently carefully sawing the rib cage open so that the heart, liver, and other organs could be carefully removed.

A series of containers were ready to receive each of the organs as they were removed. The process was handled very efficiently, and a body could be harvested in the allotted two hours unless some unique part had been requested.

He always stopped watching when it came time to skin the remains and harvest the skin tissue, the scalp, and any miscellaneous organ. It was the only time he got grossed out.

The young man that was on the table had been identified, tracked, and then brought to the warehouse and kept in a cell. He had been killed just prior to the harvesting session. This was one step that the doctor did know about.

He wondered if the good doctor recognized how fresh most of the bodies he dissected happened to be.

A few weeks later Reston received word that a second surgeon had been recruited. He informed the good doctor that he would be training the second surgeon on the harvesting procedures.

That was when he first got the word that the good doctor wanted to quit. Reston reminded the good doctor that he had made a small fortune, and that quitting was not an option.

The good doctor made the mistake of arguing with the position he was taking and threatened to expose the operation if necessary.

Reston knew immediately that he needed to take drastic and dramatic action to put the doctor back into his place.

Reston had his bodyguard do a little checking and learned that the good doctor had entered into a relationship with a surgical nurse at the hospital where he practiced. He figured that the relationship between the good doctor and the nurse was the reason for the good doctors change of heart. He came to an immediate solution.

The fact that the good doctor had more than ten million in the offshore account was probably an additional incentive to quit.

The nurse was very attractive. Reston obtained records and made note of the key DNA, blood type, and other key attributes.

He waited until the right parts request came in. He was going to snuff out the superior attitude of the good doctor. He was going to emotionally destroy him.

A few weeks later after a couple more discussions about the desire to quit, Reston took the action he knew would totally change the good doctors attitude and ensure he had control of the situation.

He had the nurse, that the good doctor was having an affair with, snatched, and brought to the warehouse.

He waited until the good doctor was ready for the next body and walked in and handed him the extensive list of parts to be harvested. The list had every organ, a knee joint, an entire right leg, eyes, and the breast nipples on it.

He wanted to be in the room when the good doctor realized who his next harvest victim happened to be.

He stepped to the far end of the room with a direct view of the operating table. He had Dennis his bodyguard standing next to him in case he needed protection.

Sara was scared as she sat in the cage and watched the two men who had snatched her from the parking lot the day before as she got ready to go home. They had not replied to any of her questions or explained why they had snatched her.

Zack and Brent had exchanged a few quiet comments about their next victim. They agreed she was too pretty to be processed but they had their orders.

Zack got the call to prepare her for the next harvest. He opened the door to the cage and let her know that she could leave the cage.

As she stepped out of the cage, Brent hit her with the knuckles of his thumb on her two temples. She went out like a light when the switch was flipped.

They lifted her and put her face down on the processing table. Brent then slit each of her arteries in her neck. He then focused on undressing her as her blood pumped out and ran down into the collection bag. The blood would be filtered and sold to a blood bank.

He admired her beautiful body and was sorry that she had been selected but that was the bosses decision not his.

When the call came to wheel the body into the harvesting room they opened the door and pushed the table in.

James asked why Reston was in the room instead of behind the observation window. He was surprised to hear that Reston say that he had a surprise for him.

James watched as the table with the harvest body was pushed into the room and put next to the dissection table. He walked over to help in rolling the body over onto the table.

There was something familiar about the body, but he could not quite place the feeling.

As the body was turned over, his brain exploded, his life was shattered. It was Sara, the woman that he had fallen in love with.

He heard Reston call out, "surprise" as he picked up his scalpel.

He took the only action that flashed into his mind.

2 The Nurse

The large panoramic screen in the living room zoomed out to the mountains, then slowly panned along the river and finally on the campsite where her father was putting up the large tent that they had all shared. Her mother had just transferred all her family videos to the cloud and wanted to view a few. The family had traveled extensively around the country and had camped in many of the national or state parks. The clip that was on the screen had been taken in a campground near the Tetons. She remembered the cold stream water where she swam briefly in a clear pool where she could see the fish swimming below her. She also remembered catching some of those fish and watching her father clean and fry them over the open campfire. At that time, she was probably fourteen. It had been one of many bright memories of growing up.

The other memory of that trip was the drive through Yellow Stone, seeing the buffalo and Old Faithful. She was sure her mother would have extensive footage of that drive as well.

She took a sip of her wine and had to admit that she had grown up in a loving family as a spoiled young girl.

Her early school years were a blur, and she had little recall about specific events.

She considered her high school years to be rather busy and exciting. She had been on the school paper, a cheer leader, and was a lettered field hockey player. Her senior year was especially fun because of all the parties she had attended. The only thing that she regretted about that time was that she had not been very serious about what she was going to do after high school.

As graduation loomed, she decided to go into nursing and was admitted to the University of Cincinnati. That made her parents happy because she would stay near home. She was excited because she felt that she had found her way into a field that felt right for her. She realized that she enjoyed helping people and thought that nursing would satisfy her desires. Her mother had suggested becoming a doctor, but Sara knew she did not have the desire nor the grade point average that would get her accepted in most US schools.

She graduated and was pleased when she was hired by the UC hospital as a practicing nurse. She was first assigned to be a floor nurse. She worked hard and received excellent feedback on her performance.

A year later she applied for and got a position as a surgical assistant. This assignment at first was a little overwhelming and watching surgery took getting used to. She at first had a quesy stomach but slowly got over it.

Then she had assisted Dr. Westin during one of his surgeries. He was fast, accurate, and seemed to have a good sense of humor.

He seemed to like her and requested her by name for several subsequent surgeries.

Their relationship seemed to take a natural turn toward intimacy.

Sara had dated James for more than a year when he asked if she would go on a vacation trip with him. She had accepted and he had asked her to pick the vacation trip that she wanted to go on. She had thought about going to Yellowstone but was not sure that camping out would be that romantic. She decided that an Alaskan cruise sponsored by one of the famous magazines on one of the smaller ships would be just the thing.

They had a main deck cabin that had an outside view. The cruise departed Seattle and for fourteen days they spent their time together. They dined each evening with a number of the guests. Sara noted that there were thirty couples on the cruise and another handful of single people for about sixty people in total. The small number of people was what had attracted her to this particular cruise.

She knew that it was rather expensive, but James had let her know that the cost was no issue.

They had enjoyed hiking, biking, kayaking at various moments, and strolling through Petersburg and learning about its fishing industry. She had followed in her mother's footsteps and used her phone to capture most of what she saw. She of course took many selfies that she sent to her parents.

The tour ended in Sitka Alaska where they caught a flight back to Cincinnati.

Sara felt that it had turned out to be fourteen of the best days of her life.

On the way back to Cincinnati, James suggested that she move in with him. She accepted on the condition that they each had their own bedroom.

He had accepted and said that he currently rented a three-bedroom apartment a few blocks from the University hospital.

They agreed that she would move in as soon as her own apartment contract ended in two months.

Her mother asked her to come to dinner and share the highlights of the vacation. Sara knew that what her mother wanted was the inside scoop on the romance.

She was eager to share that news, but she also had a great video of the highlights of the vacation that she had purchased as part of the tour. It was professionally done, and she knew her mother and dad would love it.

Sara floated along in sort of a haze as she waited for her lease to end. She went to James apartment and was amazed at how spacious and comfortable it felt. She was ready to make the move.

After work, she was walking out to her car when suddenly she was grabbed and felt a cloth going over her mouth and nose. She identified the smell of chloroform before she passed out.

When she came to she was lying in a barred cell. She sat up and tried to get her bearings. She realized that she had been kidnapped and wondered what was happening. She spent the night awake and scared.

Then the next day a person that she did not know approached the cell and told her she was going to be just fine if she did as she was told.

She asked what was going on.

The reply that everything was going to be alright did not satisfy her.

Alright meant to not have been kidnapped.

A short time later, the first person returned with a second one. He said it was time for a surprise and opened the cell door and told her to come out.

She was warry but figured that getting out of the cell was better than resisting and staying in the cell. As she stepped beyond the door, suddenly she was hit on her two temples, and everything went dark.

Zack picked up the young woman and put her on the dissection transport table. They had been instructed to undress her, bleed her, and then turn her face down before pushing the gurney into the dissection room.

He nodded when Brent commented that it was pity to have to kill such a beautiful young woman. The two of them knew better than to question the bosses direction and they did as they were told.

A few moments later they had everything ready.

3 The Doctor

All he could remember about his father were the beatings that he regularly received and the smell of alcohol as his father yelled at him for doing something wrong or being so stupid. He also remembered the beatings that his mother endured and the purple bruises on her face.

Then his father abandoned the family and things actually got better.

His mother struggled as she tried to raise five children and work to get food on the table. The food stamp program started and that at least ensured that there was food to eat but having a place to live was a struggle. They ended up living in a two-bedroom basement apartment with no windows. The saving grace was it was within three blocks of a park that had slides, swings, and a ball field.

He was the oldest and often had to take his brothers and sisters to the park and watch them. He actually enjoyed this responsibility.

He remembered his father calling him stupid, which made him focus on his schoolwork and focus on getting the best grades possible. He excelled in school and as he went through high school he targeted being the top of his class. He wanted to go to college and was hoping to get a scholarship to do so.

He was also sensitive to the fact that there was little for anything extra. He got a job at a Wendy's and was soon the lead supervisor and made a whopping nine fifty an hour. He worked twenty hours a week, mostly on weekends.

He was a loner that had few friends and in his senior year his extracurricular activity was to work in the refreshment stand which gave him a good view of the football game being played.

He hit his goal of being top in his class and accepted a full scholarship to Case Western Reserve University in Cleveland. He was excited but realized that once again he needed to be at the top of his class to enable his entry to some medical school.

The four years there was far more intense than his high school years, but he ended up as the student with the third highest grade in his class.

He had filled out requests to more than twenty medical schools. He was blown away when he received an offer from the University of Pittsburgh Medical Center (Pittsburgh, PA). He knew they were ranked # 3 in the plastic surgery field. His only concern was paying for the program and again rejoiced at receiving a stipend that went a long way to helping pay for the program.

He knew he would end up in debt but figured he would make it up when he graduated. He had researched and found out that the average salary of a plastic surgeon was three hundred fifty with a high of five hundred fifty thousand dollars a year.

The intensity of his studies increased by several multiples. He often slept at the hospital so that he would not have to go to the apartment he rented. The whirl wind seemed to last for a lifetime but then it was time to get into a residency program. He was very happy to be offered one at the University of Cincinnati hospital. This brought him back to his hometown and to his family. He however had an income issue in that his residency pay though at the top end was only seventy thousand dollars a year and with only a five thousand dollar per year increase.

Almost immediately he began looking for a moonlight job where he could leverage his degree.

He was having a night out and sitting alone at the bar talking to the bartender about his predicament. The bartender nodded and said he might have the answer to his problem. The bartender left and a few minutes later a person, who looked exactly like an Italian mafia actor from the movies came and sat next to him.

He introduced himself as Reston Sanclemente and asked him about his experience as a plastic surgeon.

James shared his scholastic and medical experience and the fact that he was almost a half a million dollars of debt and that his current pay was only seventy thousand a year.

He listened as Reston let him know that he ran a legitimate body parts business and that he was looking for a surgeon that could harvest body parts from fresh cadavers. He pointed out that it was a gory business but very lucrative.

Reston then said that if James could begin immediately he would pay fifty thousand for every cadaver that was processed and that he estimated that each harvest would only take about two hours. He needed someone willing to work six hours a week.

James was surprised and a quick calculation let him know that it was worth about four million a year. He said that he was definitely interested. He was already thinking about what that kind of money would mean for him.

Reston stipulated that James needed to finish his residency and get licensed.

James agreed and before leaving Reston took out a contract that specified everything that had been discussed and James read and signed it.

He focused on his residency, processed bodies at the facility that Reston operated and watched his bank account slowly reach twelve million.

Never in his life had he dreamt of having the kind of money that he was making. He set up a college fund for each of his brothers and sisters and moved his mother into her own home.

Over the first year he came to the realization that something about the operation seemed fishy. He began to pay attention and suspected that Reston was in fact running a body parts black market business.

He knew that he was in too deep to say anything.

Reston approached him to let him know that a second surgeon was being added to the business and that he expected him to bring him on board rapidly so that the new guy could begin contributing immediately.

James decided that it was the time to see if he could get out of the body parts business. He had a blossoming love affair going and he was coming to the end of his residency and had received his license. It was time to move on and get his personal life organized.

He mentioned that it seemed that this was a good time for him to go into his own practice and stop harvesting body parts.

He was surprised by Reston's response that leaving was not an option.

James pointed out that he had fulfilled his contract and that he intended to go into practice on his own. That was when he learned that the millions he had in an offshore account was not going to be available if he left the parts business. He then realized that Reston was a second person on the account and could block his withdrawals.

He thought that a way out was to transfer most of the money to a separate account and then quit. He had no idea what Reston had in mind. His account was blocked when he went to transfer money to another bank. He knew that he was boxed in.

He focused on his work and his new love affair. He was able to pay for the vacation that he and Sara planned. They went together on an Alaskan cruise. Each day he knew he had found the person of his dreams. It was the best time of his life. He came back eager to have Sara with him every day.

Everything seemed to be going right.

He went to his moonlight job where Reston said he had a surprise for him. He wondered what in the world Reston had in mind.

When the next body came in and he turned it over, his world ended. He could hear Reston shouting out surprise and looked down at Sara. He took his scalpel and swiftly pulled across his throat.

The world that he had dreamt about had ended for him.

4 A Day at the Waterpark

*T*he day was hot and a day at the water park seemed to be the best way to enjoy it. Alex and Matt had joined Trey, Lindsey, and Nolan for the day. They were all in the shallow end of the pool enjoying staying cool. The talk was about their last case, the fun they had in Montreal and the fact that it had been a quiet month since they had returned.

Nolan was having a great time swimming and jumping into the pool. He was content to play alone.

Then Annie arrived with Linda and Lorie, and the swimming action went into full gear.

Alex teased Annie about having increased the noise level three-fold.

Annie pointed to the table that had several bags on it and countered that she could leave but she would have to take the picnic lunch with her.

Alex laughed and said that she was ready for lunch and would set the table. Lindsey said that she would help, and they got out of the water, took a quick clean water rinse, and toweled off.

Lindsey asked what the next work assignment might be.

Alex said that the Chief had purposely not assigned them to a case and had promised that he would try to assign an easy one that might come up. She then laughed and said that was a line he had now used multiple times, but it seemed that easy cases didn't exist.

Lindsey nodded and agreed. She said that she always asked Trey about the cases that were assigned, and he always told her to relax because he had the best partner he could possibly have, and she always took care of him.

Alex smiled and replied that she felt the same about her partner.

The picnic consisted of spareribs, broccoli, asparagus, a half a corn cob and a baked potato. It was a robust meal.

Annie called everyone to get their lunch.

Alex commented that everyone must have been hungry because no one was talking.

Nolan asked who the next bad guy was.

Alex smiled and said that as soon as she knew she would make sure to tell him.

He laughed and said that the last bad guy turned out to be a woman.

Alex replied that the bad woman was one of the worst bad person that she had so far experienced.

It was at this point that her phone rang. She knew not to ignore it because it was the Chiefs' "Hail to the Chief" ring.

He began by asking how she was and what she was doing.

It was Sunday but it was clear that he was about to assign the next case. He apologized about interrupting her picnic but said that the fire department had called him with a situation that he felt she needed to address. He said that it was a gruesome situation and that she and Trey needed to get to the scene and see what to do about it. He said he would join them at the scene and then gave her the address and asked how soon she could get there.

Alex hung up and then she looked at Nolan and asked if he had called the Chief on her. He shook his head and said he didn't have his number. She then looked at Trey and said they had to go. She asked Matt to take her personal stuff back to the apartment and that she and Trey would take the car.

On the way she brought Trey up to speed about what the Chief had shared about the situation. He was meeting them at the site and would go into the warehouse with them.

When they arrived, Alex pointed out the Chief's car and pulled in behind him.

The Chief got out of his car and as he approached them apologized for ruining their weekend but said he had little choice. He explained that the fire chief had called him and said there was a locked cooler that they opened that was full of human body parts.

The fire chief called the owner of the building who claimed to run a legitimate human body parts distribution center. The fire chief then found a surgical room and what appeared to be a preparation room. This was not on the license that his staff found on file, so he had called me, and I called you because I have a bad feeling about this operation. I also called Bill and found out that he and Trevor were boating out on Lake Cumberland. I told them that they should enjoy their time and that on Monday he would bring them on board.

Alex nodded pointed to where the fire chief was standing and led the way.

The fire chief greeted her and said that he was glad to see that the Chief had called in his star detective. He warned that what he was going to show them was gory, disgusting and alarming. The owner claimed to have all the necessary paperwork but had not shown up to present it as promised.

Alex thanked him for the warning. She looked at the Chief and asked him if he had the phone number for Dr. Rogers the police coroner.

The chief replied that he did.

Alex said that even before entering the locker she already knew that she would want every body part to get verified as to its authenticity via a DNA analysis. She pointed out that in the last case that his analysis had been the key clue that had helped to solve the case.

She then said she was ready to enter the warehouse. She looked around the section of the warehouse that had been renovated. It was clear to her that one room was a holding and preparation room and a materials storage room.

She said she would wait until Dr. Rogers arrived before going into the cooler.

During this time Alex examined each of the other rooms.

When she entered the preparation room she stopped dead in her tracks. The room was clear where bodies to get dissected were prepared.

The cage that looked like a barred prison cell sent shivers down her back. The cell that looked like a prison cell clearly indicated that live people were put there.

She pointed to it and said that she thought they had uncovered a criminal operation that was killing people to get the parts that they were selling.

Across from it in the corner was what Alex surmised was a gas-powered furnace. The odor was nauseating to her.

She spotted a door to the side of the furnace and led the way in. She was surprised to find that it was an office area. She was more surprised to find a viewing window into the surgical room. She noted that it gave the viewer a direct view across the operating table.

She pointed out that whoever sat at the comfortable chair in front of the window must be a mentally sick person.

The surgical room looked like any well-equipped hospital surgery room, but it did not have any of the equipment associated with helping keep someone alive.

Dr. Rogers arrived after about an hour.

She was in the surgical room looking at the observation window that from the surgical room looked like a mirror when Dr. Rogers approached her.

Alex greeted him and said that she was asking him to take the lead in examining the body parts in the freezer.

He nodded and replied that every case that he worked for her seemed to get weirder. He asked how much weirder this one might be.

Alex said that she had no clue.

She followed Dr. Rogers in and realized that it was not a freezer or as cold as she expected. Many of the body parts were each sealed in what looked like evacuated plastic bags and there were a number of cooler like containers that she figured held specific body parts.

It was a gruesome site.

Alex took a quick look around and was amazed at all the body parts. She did not take a count but was sure there were hundreds.

She shook her head and said she had seen enough and walked out.

She recalled seeing the body parts of what had appeared to be that of a child. Now her heart stopped as she looked at the cell with a vision of a kidnapped child sitting there.

She shook her head and said that she wanted an arrest warrant put out for the owner of the warehouse and for anyone on record that worked at the facility. She was going to grill them on what might have transpired at the facility.

The Chief nodded and said that he agreed with her and that the next step would be to identify the people she had mentioned and bring them in for questioning.

He took out his phone and made several calls asking that warrants be issued for everyone listed on the warehouse records.

Alex turned to Trey and asked him about his feelings about what they had seen.

Trey shook his head and said that the case seemed to be taking a tack into a very weird world that he had never envisioned. He agreed that they might have uncovered a situation that was more than a nightmare and in a way worse than their last case.

Alex agreed. She said that she was ready to leave. She asked what he planned to do.

Trey made a call and found out that Lesley, Noland, Annie and her two were at his house. He hung up and replied that he was going home, have a beer and watch the kids play and try to forget what they had just witnessed.

Alex asked him to drop her off. She said that Matt had the rest of the day off. She was going to see if he would go out on a bike ride with her otherwise she would have to get on the treadmill and run for the rest of the day to help her release the tension that had built up.

The following Monday Alex and Johnnie arrived at the office and found Bob and Travis sitting at their desks and a box of donuts on her desk.

Travis greeted her and said that he had been warned by Bob not to open the box and let the Boss take her roll first.

Bob piped up and said that he had not issued any warning and that it was Travis's idea to wait for the boss. They both chuckled and said that they were eager to hear about the new assignment that they were all on. They commented that they had each received a call from the Chief and had been brought on board and that they would all be on the quest to solve the mystery of the fire at the warehouses and determine the legitimacy of the human body parts business.

Alex opened the box and took out a bear claw, cut it in half, and put half on Trey's desk. She was aware that Trey was later than normal and was about to call when he walked in with his cup of coffee.

Trey greeted everyone and then said that he was late because he had stopped to interview for a door greeters job at the lumber yard.

Alex smiled and told him he would be a failure in that role because he would scare away the customers. His comment worried her, but she would make sure Trey was OK later.. The two of them would be attending the AA meeting together the next evening. She was sure she would know if he was doing alright.

She was about to suggest that they go into a huddle room to discuss the case when the Chief walked in and said that he would like to talk to all of them in his office.

Alex noted that the rest of the people in the bullpen were all watching them closely.

The Chief sat behind his desk holding a cup of coffee. He made the comment that it seemed that lately each case got weirder than the previous one. He then added that he was once again putting two teams on the case because they seemed to work well together, and they solved cases. He asked if that suited everyone.

Travis smiled and commented that they didn't have a choice but to work well together because he just couldn't stand to see Alex cry.

Alex smiled and replied that she would make sure that he got the best assignment for being so sensitive to her feelings. She knew full well that Travis had become one of her supporters.

The Chief nodded, said that he was sure they could work it out and then explained the details of the case as he understood it.

The fire chief had called him and let him know that the fire had been purposely set. A loose connection had been found on the cremation furnace and a short time later they had found the charred remains of a stick with the wick that most likely contained gas or some other flammable. The fire chief has the evidence secured and he said that the crime scene was taped off and was under twenty-four-hour watch.

He then shared the fact that Dr. Rogers had his teamwork working around the clock to move all the body parts into the morgue and he had worked over the weekend to get started in processing the body parts.

He looked at Alex and asked how she was thinking to approach the case.

Alex nodded her head and said that she wanted to get the team to discuss the case in a little more detail before deciding on the approach. She made the point that the proprietor seemed to have skipped, other members such as the person doing the dissection, and any helpers were unknowns and now an arsonist had been added to the list. This meant that there were multiple scenarios that needed to be addressed.

She suggested going to the morgue and getting Dr. Rogers to take on what the case. She added that he would have the best take on the body parts. Then they might talk to the Fire Chief to see if he had an ideas who the arsonist might be.

She added that when they found him they might need to give that person a metal.

The Chief nodded and picked up the phone and made a call. He asked if his team could come to the morgue and get an update on what the doctor had found out.

He stood up and said they should all go down to the lab.

Alex did not like the smell of the morgue. It made her nauseous. When they entered there was a full leg on the table that was obviously a woman's leg. It sent a shiver down her back.

The doctor pointed it out and said that he had started with the largest of the body parts, was running the analysis and was about ready to put the sample back in the bag that it had come in.

Alex asked how long it would take to process all the body parts.

Dr. Rogers replied that it would most likely take the rest of the week.

Alex nodded and then asked what type of information would each analysis give them.

The reply was that they would get DNA, blood type, approximate age of the individual, and that he would add any additional information that he had from the observation of each part. He made the point that they had already concluded that the person doing the body part harvesting was a skilled surgeon.

Alex thanked him and asked him to send up each report individually so that the team could begin to use the information to hunt down who the person might be.

She then turned and said it was time to go to their huddle room and discuss the case.

5 New Digs, New Staff, New Business

The night was dark, and the Cheshire moon seemed to be mocking him as he lay on his sleeping bag looking up at the sky. He had abandoned his apartment and planned to leave the area, but he was thinking through how he could slow down the hunt for him that he was sure to follow. He had learned from one of his informants that the top detective and from the press she received that she did a very thorough investigation and always seemed to catch the person she was after.

He made up his mind that she needed to be killed. He figured that then there would be a lengthy delay, and he would be able to disappear and reappear as a different individual.

He decided to have Dennis, his eager bodyguard, take a shot at taking her out. He knew that Dennis was always wanting to shoot someone, and this opportunity would attract him. He would ask Zack and Brent to back Dennis up.

He figured the three of them had a good chance a getting the job done. If they were successful he felt he had a chance to relocate his operation somewhere outside of Cincinnati but still along the main path to the East coast body distribution thoroughfare.

He knew that he had to do so rapidly or face the ire of his bosses in Italy.

He knew that the paperwork he had that normally was sufficient to make the operation look legitimate would not stand close scrutiny. He hoped that most of the body parts would be impossible to trace but he worried about how good the coroner might be. He was sure most of the body parts would be impossible to trace. He had the records of who the persons were. These were records he had matched to the customer needs.

He kept wondering how the fire had started. It seemed that when he drove by that the fire was in the area where the preparation and surgery room was located. He thought about what supplies were stored in that area, and he went through the list of the chemicals stored there. There were cleaning supplies that were flammable, but he had his people store them in a separate area. He thought about the gas lines that came to a small cremation oven where the discarded body parts were cut up and cremated. He felt that it must have been a gas leak of some kind. He would watch the news to see if the fire department made their findings public.

The next morning, he used one his burner phones and called Dennis and asked him to meet him at the Hamilton County Park so they could plan on what to do.

Dennis was excited about the job of taking out "Cincinnati's Black Annie Oakley." He said she didn't stand a chance.

Reston reminded him that she was a dead shot and that several other folks had tried unsuccessfully to kill her.

Dennis smiled and said he did not intend to play fair and that he would shoot her in the back.

Reston asked him to contact Zack and Brent and get them to help him and said there was a ten-thousand-dollar bonus for each of them.

He personally and desperately hoped that Dennis would be successful.

He gave Dennis the building address where the black detective lived and let Dennis know that she rode a bicycle into work early every morning and suggested that he observe her for a couple of days so he could decide when and how to shoot her.

Dennis said that his three fifty-seven would blow a hole the size of a basketball as it left her body. He commented that she would be dead before she hit the ground.

Reston worried about Dennis's self-confidence, but he knew that Dennis was a dead shot and would probably not miss.

He suggested that Dennis buy a getaway car and gave him the name of the dealer he knew had a bunch of cars that were in relatively good condition.

He went to that used car lot, purchased an older Hyundai, and drove slowly toward Cleveland. It was a long drive and on the way he contemplated how he would set up the business in Cleveland.

He took a room at a Motel for the week. He was going to move slowly and keep his ears to the ground to see what would happen.

He transferred some of the money from the Jamaican bank account that he had set up with James his use-to-be plastic surgeon that was now in the body parts cooler. The twelve million was down to a little under eight million because James had set up a series of trust accounts for his brothers, sisters, and his mother. Reston had been aware of the setting up of the trust accounts and had actually thought that was the right thing for James to do.

As it turned out, when James had turned over the body of his fiancé on the parts table and had then slit his own throat it had startled him, but it turned out it was good that he had done so.

He had the new surgeon do the dissection and a few days later the fire had ended the business.

He could not sit in his room, so he spent the next couple of days going to a local pub and nursing drinks and listening to the news broadcasts. He was a little disappointed about the lack of information about the fire in the warehouse. The only thing that had been reported was that the fire seemed to have been purposely set. That just didn't make sense.

He wished he could take a walk through the warehouse to get a firsthand look. He wondered who would have wanted to set the place on fire.

He wondered how Dennis was doing and decided to give him a call.

His call gave him hope that things would improve.

Dennis said that he had watched the black detective leave her place for the last three days and knew exactly how he would take her out. He said that she was a dead woman walking but just didn't know it.

It was uplifting to hear the enthusiasm and the certainty that Dennis was exuding. He reminded Dennis to be careful and have his getaway planned. He suggested he call when the job was done, and he had made his getaway.

Dennis took his two helpers on a walk to show them where they would wait the next morning and that they both should plan to wait for him to shoot but then shoot away to make sure that both she and her partner bike rider were dead. He said that he had the getaway car parked so that they would drive and get on US Highway Seventy-One north and drive north to Cleveland. He let them know about the thirty-thousand-dollar reward.

Zack said that it seemed easy enough and that he was sure they would be enjoying the reward.

The next morning the three were standing in the dark leaning against the apartment wall when Dennis heard the apartment door slide open. He had his three fifty-seven in his hand and as the detective was getting ready to mount her bike he fired three shots. He smiled as she was hurled forward but was stunned as she seemed to turn in midair and fire. Then the world ended.

Reston was stunned by the breaking news report that highlighted the fact that Cincinnati's most famous detective was in the hospital where she was being treated for a non-life-threatening gunshot wound. The reporter went on to say that she had killed two shooters and that her partner had killed a third. An apparent getaway car was found parked in the garage across from the apartment, which was the home of the detective.

The camera scene then showed three body bags that were getting ready to be loaded into the coroner's van.

Reston knew that he would need to find a long-term hiding place and sent word to his bosses that the body parts business in Cincinnati had been disrupted.

His bosses told him he was to hide in plain sight and open up a new body parts factory in either Columbus or in Cleveland. They suggested Cleveland because they had a better network there and they had informants in the police department and several of the political offices.

Reston didn't like it, but he knew he was toast if he declined. He changed his identity to Preston Clemente. This was a passport that he had obtain a few years prior. Then he found an apartment that had a view of the lake in a relatively prestigious area. Once he had set himself up in the apartment he went about finding an appropriate warehouse or building to use.

He went out personally and drove around various areas and found a shuttered three-story home that sat on the corner of a sleepy street not far from the lake. He took the time to visit the place several times under different weather conditions to ensure that there was always a good lake breeze. He wanted to make sure that his cremation furnace would not draw any attention. He then looked up the owner of the property and negotiated the sale. It was an easy one because the house had been unused for almost a year.

He then contacted his associates and asked them to recruit the harvesting surgeon and to provide him with three capable associates. He specified that one needed to be a bodyguard that was good with his weapon and had experience.

He also asked to be referred to the appropriate contractor that could come in and prepare the house for use.

He had the operating room on the second floor, the holding room, and the parts cooler on the first floor and the cremation oven in the basement. He put his observation room on the third floor with the viewing port through the floor. An elevator made the multilevel operation a convenient one.

One side of the house had an empty lot that he bought, and he made an enticing offer for the small home on the other side so that he had a buffer all the way around the building.

It was less than a month later that he was ready to begin his new body harvesting business.

His bosses congratulated him on getting back into business and gave him the names of the three persons that would be working for him. They would drive in from New York.

He hoped that the three would work out.

It turned out that the three were fresh from the home country and eager do what he asked. He offered to house them gratis at the small house next door and worked with them to get the house ready for their occupancy.

He went with all of them to a local gun range and was impressed with their shooting skill. He discussed how the body parts business was run and learned that all three were comfortable with how it operated and how the people that might become parts were selected.

He took them all out to celebrate.

He liked all three.

Luca was the bodyguard, but he said that he was willing to do whatever he might be asked to do.

Angelo and Dario were both darker individuals that said the they had no qualms at getting the bodies ready for dissection.

They all asked whether they could trust the surgeon that would be doing the dissecting.

Reston replied that he had not met the surgeon, but he was counting on the family to provide the surgeon that they had vetted, and the surgeon would also be coming from Italy via New York.

<u>6 The Magician</u>

Johnnie was disturbed by the new case. It seemed unreal. He had never imagined a business focused on making a profit from human body parts. When the team had gone to the morgue where Dr. Rogers was working his way through the body parts and getting the DNA signature and other metrics from each part. The doctor had joked about starting with the best-looking body part which was an entire female right leg. He pointed to a row of refrigerated drawers and said that his team had moved all the parts from the warehouse cooler shelves and put them in the top row. He had only gotten everything organized and had the result of only the leg.

He listened to Alex thank the doctor and asked that the information be sent to her so that the team could begin trying to verify whether it was a legitimate body part.

When the team was back in the huddle room he admitted that he was not sure what databases he would need to access to verify a body part.

They had all agreed with Alex that they would work together to get organized and get ideas on how they were going to verify all the parts. She pointed out that the listed business owner had not delivered the paperwork as he had promised and when she checked his given address it was a fake. She figured that the business was probably a black market one.

They discussed the assignment for a short time and then Alex had suggested they call it a day and go relieve the tensions of the day.

The next morning, he greeted Alex as she got off the elevator with her bike. He could tell by her looks that she had not gotten the best sleep. He led the way out of the building. He was just getting ready to get on his bike when the roar of gunfire cause him to drop his bike, pull his pistol and drop prone on the ground. He watched as Alex flew over her bike, spun in the air, and fired her gun four times and then hit the pavement. She had hit two of the three attackers, and he took out the third and put an insurance shot in the second shooter. It was clear to him that Alex had nailed the person who had done the shooting. All three of the shooters were down.

He jumped up ran to make sure that all three were dead and kicked their guns to their feet. He then spun and ran to where Alex was lying face up, but it was clear to him that she was out. He check for a pulse and was ecstatic to find a strong one. He quickly dialed the dispatch center and declare that there was an officer down and gave the address.

It seemed that he heard the sirens immediately after that. He was focused on trying to see what condition Alex was in. He rolled her to her side and saw that she had indeed been hit and was bleeding. He jumped over to his bike and got his first aid kit. With his pocketknife he cut the straps on the backpack that Alex had on and cut open the back of her blouse to expose the wound. He was surprised to see the exposed back of a bullet. He wiped the blood away and put his largest band aid over it. There was another wound along her right shoulder on which he sprayed a sealing adhesive with pain killer.

Suddenly it seemed that he was surrounded by police and an EMT pulled him away from Alex and said that they would take her to the hospital. He sat back on the curb and watched Alex being loaded onto the stretcher and then into the ambulance. He watched it pull away and then turned to look at the scene.

His bike was OK, but Alex's bike had a bent back wheel that would need to be replaced. He was about to pick up his first aid kit when one of the police officers said that he should leave everything alone and asked him what had happened.

Johnnie stood up and pointed to the three bodies and said that he and Alex had come out of the building with their bikes and were just getting ready to take off when the roar of gunfire started. He described what Alex had done and then what he had done. He pointed to the weapons that the three attackers were using and said that it was a wonder that Alex was alive because all three were using three-fifty-sevens.

He said that he thought the only one that had gotten any shots off was the one that was in the lead position. Alex had nailed him, and the second person and he had taken out the third shooter, and he had also put a shot into the second shooter for insurance.

The coroner's van arrived a few moments later and a couple of his people took pictures, asked almost the same questions that Johnnie had already answered and then put the bodies into bags and put them in the van. The van drove off but Dr. Stevens and one of his team continued to work the crime scene.

The Chief arrived and rescued him. The Chief let the officer in charge know that he was taking Johnnie to the station. Trey stopped them and asked about Alex.

The Chief said he had been told that she was still out and that she was being kept that way until she got out of surgery. She had a flattened three-fifty-seven bullet that had lodged in her right back muscle and a graze wound across her shoulder. It seems that the two computers and a one-inch-thick spiral binder that had been in the backpack had saved her.

The Chief shared the fact that both computers and the binder had an almost one-inch hole through them, and the top computer had a groove across it that was most likely made by another bullet that caused her shoulder wound. The surgeon said that he had never treated a patient that had survived getting shot by such a weapon.

The Chief went on to share that the field team was still looking for the third bullet. He figured they would continue looking until they found it.

Trey said that he was going to the hospital to be there when Alex woke up.

The Chief nodded and said that they would all go there together.

They were not surprised to see Matt waiting outside of Alex's intensive care room. He let them know that she was still in the resuscitation area recovering from surgery but would soon be moved into the room where he was standing.

She was going to be kept out for most of the rest of the day because she had hit her head on the pavement and had a slight concussion.

Trey suggested that they go back to the station and let Matt contact them when Alex was awake. They could begin to try and figure out who the three shooters were, and who they might be working for. He also wanted to get a better understanding of how Alex had survived being shot by such a powerful weapon. He said he believed in miracles because he had experienced several in his work with Alex. He was just very happy about the current miracle that had saved Alex.

When they returned to the station, the Chief called down to the coroner's lab and learned that the backpack that Alex had on when she was shot was on his table and he was about to examine in. He said that the three bodies were in the cooler and would be processed in due time. He figured that they were not as important a figuring out how Alex had survived being shot by a three-fifty-seven.

He added that they had found the third bullet buried just past where Alex had landed. He speculated that the third shot was fired as the shooter died.

They all took the elevator down to the morgue where they were greeted by Dr. Rogers. He said that he had gotten word that Alex was going to recover but would have a couple of scars on her back. He pointed to the table where he had systematically unpacked the backpack she had on when she had been shot.

He said that the backpack buckle, the two computers and the one-inch-thick spiral binder had all partnered to slow the bullet enough so that it flattened and then only had enough power left to lodge a half an inch into her back muscle. He then pointed to the grove that went lengthwise along the first computer and said that the second shot must have occurred as she was being flung forward and the bullet hit the computer and was deflected. He said that three shots had been fired by the shooter, and his team had found it in the blacktop pavement.

He pointed at the notebook and asked when she had started to use it because it had Johnnie's name on it and had only some cryptic notes on the first few pages.

Johnnies smiled and shared that he had given Alex the notebook the evening before because she wanted to make a few notes for the next day. The two of them had been discussing what databases he should be looking in to verify the legitimacy of all the body parts.

Dr. Rogers nodded and said that the notebook was probably the key in sapping the bullets energy because the computers were light laptops that did not have much structural resistance.

Johnnie asked permission to take a picture of the page that had the notes that Alex had written.

Trey commented that Alex had switched from having her cars blown up and burned to having computers destroyed.

The Chief nodded and agreed and then added that it was much easier on his budget to replace the computers than to replace the police cars that she had gone through.

Trey suggested that he and Johnnie join Bob and Travis, enjoy a cup of coffee, and then dig into the case and see if they could make some headway that they could share with Alex when she came out of her sedation.

Bob and Travis were sitting at their desks and the fact that they each had two donuts that they were munching on at the same time showed that both were nervous or upset.

Travis looked at Johnnie and asked how he could have let her get shot.

Johnnie smiled and used the reply that he had heard Alex often give Travis of, "I love you too."

Bill simply said, "touche."

Trey took out a bear claw and said he was going to eat Alex's half for her, and he was going to insist they all go into the huddle room and work together to see if they could take the next few steps without her.

7 The Evil Place

Joshua had taken the job because it offered good pay, and he could do the cleaning and sweeping at night. This allowed him to hold two jobs. He needed both jobs to take care of his family and his ailing mother. He went about his new job with enthusiasm and a desire to do a great job.

He had agreed to take cash for the work and was very happy about the pay that was twice as much as what he made during the day.

He felt that his angels were looking out for him.

But after a few days he began to take notice of the place. Most of the warehouse was empty and did not need cleaning. The part cleaned put him on edge. It had seemed too good to be true and as he looked at the area he was cleaning he became alarmed. He wondered about the cage like a jail cell. The room that the cage was in also had a small furnace in the other corner that had a weird odor to it, and there were two tables on wheels that had trough like edges with a drainpipe on one side.

The room gave him goose bumps and literally spooked him.

The next room alarmed him. He was sure that the stainless-steel table was an operating table but there was not equipment to keep people alive.

He saw the mirror that seemed to provide a way to look into the room. He searched out the entrance to what he was sure would be an observation room and found it. He went in and knew he had taken a job that was involved in evil.

He looked around at the room and concluded that whoever sat there was probably in charge of the place because the room was set up to be comfortable. It had a small refrigerator, a small countertop oven and a shelf with a variety of liquor bottles. The small sink had two glasses that were open side down on a towel.

He returned to the room with the operating table and saw a locked door that had a small glass window across the room. He went over and looked through it and almost fainted. He had to hold on to the handle to keep from passing out. He knew he could pick the lock but was afraid to step into the room where he saw a variety of body parts. He figured he had found the door to hell and immediately let go as if the handle had burned his hands.

He finished his cleaning and got out of the warehouse. He vowed to that he would never come back.

What he had seen kept nagging him. He knew he should go to the police, but he was afraid of being exposed. He knew that the person running the place was the devil incarnate and would have him killed and he might end up in the room on the other side of the little window.

He remembered the various items in the place and figured that a gas explosion and fire might end the operation.

The thought would not leave him. He thought through how he could carry out what came to mind and prepared to do it. He figure he needed a couple of vise grips, and he needed an ignition source.

He got everything together and returned the following evening. He had no plan to do any cleaning. He was there to destroy the place.

He went to the window in the room located just behind the holding cell that opened to the ground above and pushed it open a few inches. Then he went to the gas line that went to the oven and loosened the connection until he could smell the gas coming out. He left the area, went outside, and went to the window that he had opened.

When he smelled the gas, he lit the small gas-soaked torch that he had made and threw it in through the window. As soon as he had thrown in the torch the explosion blew out the window. He had expected that and had located himself off to the side.

He got up and quickly walked to his car that was parked two blocks away. He could hear the sirens blaring as he slowly left the area. He hoped that the fire crew would not be able to save the place.

He knew that he would need to look for another job, but his soul was lifted by the fact that he had taken out the macabre and evil business.

Now all he had to do was to find another job. He would have to see if one of the fast-food places needed help. It would not pay what he had made for the last few weeks, but he could rest easy and have a clear conscience.

He followed the news and learned that the fire department had determined that the fire had been deliberately set and they were looking for the arsonist that had set it. They had no clue who had set the fire, but they were asking if anyone had information that might help the investigation that was getting underway.

Trey got the news from the fire chief, and the team discussed the fact that there was some unknown person who had something against human body parts trafficking. They put finding him or her on their list of things that needed investigation but they all agreed that they had little energy in trying to track the person down.

He asked if Bob and Travis would take on the search for the person setting the fire and that if they found him they should treat him to a steak dinner at Johnnies favorite restaurant. He figure that person should be treated like a hero.

Travis smiled and said that it was one of the few times he agreed about how a suspect should be treated.

Bob added his normal brief, "Ditto."

Johnnie agreed and said he would personally pay for the dinner, and they should all focus on identifying the body parts and in catching the person that ran the body parts business.

8 Return

*A*lex was lying face down with her head turned to the side. She could hear the surgeon's comments about the bullet he was removing from her back. He kept mumbling how amazing that she had been shot twice by a three-fifty-seven and she had only a flesh wound and a grazed shoulder wound.

His assistant replied that it was a miracle but that she had also suffered a concussion from hitting her head on the pavement.

Alex wondered if they knew that she was awake and listening. Then the world seemed to become fuzzy, and she could not make out what was being said. She felt herself being lifted and moved onto a surface that seemed softer and warmer than the operation table.

She kept going between being able to hear and then going back to dreams. She replayed rescuing Annie and the two girls and there seemed to snippets from almost every case that she and the team had been on.

There seemed to be someone holding her hand, but she could not respond.

She decided to relax.

Matt had gone to the recovery room and held Alex's hand. When he felt Alex fall asleep he let go.

Not long after the nurse let him know that the doctor had given the order to move Alex to the intensive care room where she would be for the next couple of days.

Matt was relieved that the Dr. planned to keep her for a few days. He called and let Trey know that it would most likely be the next day before she would be awake and ready for any visitors.

Once Alex had been moved, he realized how exhausted he was and decided to go back to the apartment and get a good night's sleep.

As he walked out, he was pleased to see that the room had two police standing guard at Alex's door.

He had moved in with Alex and when he arrived at the apartment building he was surprised that it was still cordoned off and that there were two police officers watching the scene. All the physical evidence was gone but yellow outlines of everything was still at the scene. One of the officers recognized him and asked how Alex was doing.

He let them know that the operation to remove the bullet had gone well and that she was in an intensive care room and that some of their buddies were guarding it.

He went in and stopped by Johnnie's room and knocked on the door.

Johnnie had just hung up from talking to Mary and letting her know about the shooting and explaining that Alex had survived being shot because of what was in her backpack and how glad he had given her his biggest spiral bound notebook that was being identified as the object that most likely saved her.

Then he heard the knock and went to see who was stopping by.

He let Matt in and told him he looked like shit.

Matt said that he felt that way too.

Johnnie asked if he wanted something to drink.

Matt said he would love a shot of whiskey, but he had given up drinking and said he had just dropped by to let him know that Alex was still sleeping it off but that she was in an intensive care room and would probably be there for a couple of days.

Johnnie thanked him for the update and suggested that he go take a shower and get to bed.

Matt left and went up to the apartment.

Johnnie returned to the table where he had his computer linked up with the local hospital databases. He had no problem in hacking into any of the hospital systems. He was following the notes that Alex had put in the notebook. She had suggested comparing any report they got from Dr. Rogers to the DNA in the hospital databases.

He had gone through several of the hospital databases when he got a hit. It turned out to be that of a nurse who was a surgery assistant. He switched over to the departments missing persons reports and found her listed as missing by her worried parents. He had a hunch and tried to see if there were any missing doctors. He got another hit.

He decided that the next day he would see if Trey would follow up on the two missing persons reports and he would see if Dr. Rogers could process some of the male body parts.

He realized that the day had sapped his energy, and he went to bed earlier than usual.

The rattle of the alarm seemed to come only moments after he had fallen asleep.

He got up and decided to skip breakfast and go for a couple of donuts and a strong cup of coffee at the station. He was going to get his bike off the porch when he remembered that it was currently being held as evidence. He walked out of his apartment with the thought of having to walk to work.

The two police who had the night shift were just getting ready to leave and asked him if he wanted a ride to the station.

He replied that he would love a ride.

Once at the station he walked into the bullpen with his cup of coffee in hand and realized that he was the very first person to show and there were no donuts at hand.

He went to one of the vending machines and purchased an egg mac muffin and bacon sandwich. He threw it in the microwave for two minutes and then went back to his desk and relaxed as he ate the sandwich and sipped on his coffee.

He had just turned on his computer when Trey walked in with a cup of coffee in hand and sat down at his desk. Trey asked how the night had gone and gave a small laugh when Johnnie just grunted.

He commented that his night also deserved only a grunt.

Bob and Travis came in carrying their morning offering of assorted donuts.

Johnnie thanked them for saving his day as he took out two heavily sugar-coated cake donuts.

He shared that he had learned that the female legs and arms were that of a missing surgical nurse who had been reported missing by her parents. He said that Trey needed to get Dr. Steves to process the male parts because he had also found that one of the hospital surgeons was also listed as missing.

Trey said that as soon as the team was in the huddle room he would call down and see if Dr. Rogers would concentrate on the male body parts.

Johnnie nodded and said that he was ready for any additional reports that were available.

The Chief came in and walked over to them and commented that they all looked like he felt. He looked into the box of donuts and took a blue berry muffin and took a big bite out of it. Then he asked if there was anything that he could do.

Trey thanked him and said the team was going to go to a huddle room and figure out what they needed to do next.

The Chief turned to this office and said that he was going to get a few winks to make up for a sleepless night and they should do whatever they needed to do and order in lunch if that would be of any help.

Johnnie spoke up and said that by noon he thought he would want to eat at their favorite Asian restaurant and have Manchurian beef on a bed of rice with a mixed vegetable.

Trey said that he was in and was joined by Travis and Bill.

After lunch, the four of them decided to go and see how Alex was doing.

Trey led the way to the room and was not surprised to see Matt sitting and holding Alex's hand.

Earlier the nurse had come in to check Alex vitals when she was surprised by being asked the time.

Alex came awake as someone approached the bed. She quickly realized she was in a hospital bed and was laying on her right side. She immediately remembered the shooting and the operation on her back. She knew that she had killed two of the three shooters.

She wondered who had shot the third person. She realized that it had to be Johnnie, but she had not realized that he carried a gun. She hoped that he was OK.

When the nurse let her know it was five in the morning. She decided to get some more sleep and closed her eyes.

She opened them when breakfast was delivered but the strawberry Jell-o tasted weak, and the buttered bread and the blueberry desert did not taste good either. She decided to see what the lunch menu might offer.

She wondered how long she was going to be in the hospital.

She smiled and waved Matt over when he walked in. She gave him a kiss and said that she hoped he had not been the one to bring her to the hospital.

Matt handed her a small bag and said that it was her favorite morning treat.

Alex looked in and smiled when she saw that it was a bear claw. It smelled great. She had not poured her coffee that was on her breakfast tray but did so now and then took a healthy bite of the bear claw. She thanked Matt and said that he had helped start her day.

She then asked again if his team had brought her to the hospital.

Matt smiled at the question and shook his head. He said when the call came in about an officer down and the apartment building address was given he almost lost it, but his team was transporting an injured minor whose two parents had just been killed to Children's Hospital. He told her that the team that took her to the hospital was at the station taking a break and were on the scene in less than two minutes and they had her in the ER in less than five minutes.

That team said that Johnnie had cut off her backpack and had applied a huge band aid over the bullet and had sprayed the area that had been grazed by one of the bullets with a sealant. Their team only did the transport.

My team and I showed up about ten minutes later. I stayed and the team went out and worked the rest of the shift one person short.

Alex asked whether he had held her hand during that time.

He smiled and said that he held her hand until she fell asleep after surgery and then for a short time in the room until the nurse on duty suggested he go home and get some sleep.

Alex asked about the shooters and learned that she had killed two of three shooters and that Johnnie had killed the third one.

She smiled and said that Johnnie was fearless and once again he had helped take out the bad guys. She commented that she had not known that he was carrying a weapon.

Matt shook his head and said that was a question that she would have to ask Johnnie and Trey because he had no knowledge of most of the details of what had happened at the site of the shootout.

The two of them chatted the morning away and the lunch tray arrived, and they both commented about the bland selection.

Then a very serious looking Trey followed by a tired looking Johnnie then Bob and Travis entered the room. Johnnie moved most of the things off her tray and arranged her favorite Mongolian beef with brown rice and sweet and sour vegetables on the side.

The smell immediately made her hungry.

Johnnie then handed Matt several small containers that he said was a similar mix but with scallops.

Matt thanked him and said that Alex had all sorts of questions about what had happened that he had no clue how to answer.

Trey looked a Alex and told her to ask away.

Trevor smiled and said that he was pleased to be working with a woman who could take a three-fifty-seven bullet in the back and still kill the shooters.

Alex smiled and replied that, "she loved him too." Then she looked at Johnnie and asked when he had started carrying a weapon.

Johnnie smiled and said that his hover craft, Gunjfor, was not using her weapon, so he had qualified at the firing range and had a legal license to carry her weapon for her.

Alex asked him if he had taken out the third shooter.

Johnnie said that he had, and he had put a shot through the heart of the second shooter. He then said that only the first shooter had gotten any shots off and he had hit her with two shots and the third shot miss completely. He figured that her first shot had killed him, and his third shot was a dying reaction.

Alex smiled and asked if Johnnie thought that a band aid was all that she needed for a bullet in the back.

Johnnie chuckled and said that, and a little sealing spray on the minor bullet graze seemed to be the right thing to do and it was all he had in his emergency kit. He said that he had started carrying the emergency kit after their bike ride along the Loveland bike trail where she had been shot and kept on running toward the shooter with blood running down her arm.

Alex laughed and said that the only reason that she had run toward the shooter was because she saw a crazy old, unarmed Vietnam vet running toward the same shooter crazily shouting insults and waving his hands in the air.

Johnnie nodded and replied that being around her always seemed to draw out the most amazing events. He said that the roar of a three-fifty-seven being fired not more than twenty feet away and watching her fly with bicycle in hand and then spinning around and firing two kill shots was about as amazing as it could get. To then find her alive was for him just a plain miracle.

Alex shook her head and agreed that it was a miracle. Then she added that she had learned that it was that huge almost two-inch-thick spiral bound notebook that he had given her when she asked for a piece of paper that saved her life. She added that the surgeon had wondered where the paper that he had found in the wound had come from. He had commented that the paper seemed to have acted as a cushioning agent.

Johnnie smiled and said that he had just decided not to charge her for the notebook.

The attending doctor had been standing and listening to the banter and said that he wanted to interrupt for just a moment and ask how Alex was feeling.

Alex replied that after eating a decent lunch she was feeling great.

The doctor looked at the tray table and said that he was glad that the Chinese lunch that he had ordered had satisfied her.

Alex smiled and thanked him for being so considerate.

He nodded and said that he would order her dismissal for the coming morning. He wanted just one more day of detailed monitoring and he wanted the psychologist to come in and talk with her to make sure there was not any brain damage.

Trevor spoke up and said that there could not be any more damage because that had already happened and there was little hope of it getting any better.

The Dr. shook his head and said that he wished everyone a good day as he walked out.

Trey spoke up and said let Alex know that the team seemed to be making progress, but the case was taking a weird turn. Bob and Trevor were trying to locate an arsonist who had set the fire. They were not sure of the motive.

Johnnie was on the trail of the female body parts and had determined she had been a surgical nurse who had been reported as missing and that her fiancé surgeon was also missing. This was a twist that he had not expected. He went on and let her know that Dr. Rogers was currently processing the male body parts that fit the surgeon's size.

Alex shook her head and said that everything about the case was weird. She asked that the profit picture for such a venture and the money that all the body parts represented needed to be calculated. She figured if the profit was big enough, then the operation would be set up again and it would be somewhere nearby.

Johnnie said he could put that information together that afternoon. He would also start to gather the missing person reports for nearby cities like Louisville, Indianapolis, Dayton, Columbus, Cleveland, and Pittsburg.

He figured that every body part that they had in their possession needed to be replaced and delivered to a buyer. This meant that the missing persons would have the same makeup of the current body parts.

Alex shook her head in agreement and added that the person or persons perpetrating such a ghoulish crime had no idea about the old hound that was on their trail.

Trey laughed and added that it was good to have Alex back in the mix, but she should take it easy because they all had her back.

9 New Operation

Reston, now going by the name of Preston Clemente, walked through his new operation and was proud of having re-established an operation in less than two months.

He went through his previous parts list and confirmed the body parts that were still wanted. He used his previous list to get the DNA and other vital metrics of the parts that remained on order. About eighty percent of his list remained on order. His contacts with a variety of local doctors soon had him zeroing in on the potential donors.

His new helpers had no qualms about the gathering of the right "donors" and bringing them in for processing.

He had several satellite helpers such as a realtor, a used car lot owner and a person in the county records office that would help in disappearing those individuals that lived alone.

The realtor helped in getting any home either on the market to generate cash or off the market.

The used car owner was great at processing and selling a vehicle that the "donor" might possess.

The person in the records office provided an avenue to get a deed changed over to new ownership of a property.

The surgeon was sufficiently skilled to do the dissection, but he had lost his license for his sloppy surgical performance that had killed several of his patients. He was over a million dollars in debt to several families because he had lost the cases that had been brought against him.

Reston actually preferred him to either of his previous surgeons because dissection was his only job and he had been willing to work for a lot less and was only making as much as each of his other employees. Even so he was still making close to three hundred thousand a year and his debt was being reduced by one hundred thousand a year as a bonus. This seemed to currently satisfy him.

Reston was sure that greed would soon cause him to ask for more. He figured he had a lot of room to keep satisfying the doctor for years to come.

The operation started slowly but seemed to be ramping up smoothly.

He had heard nothing from the Cincinnati end since his henchmen had failed and had been killed. He was sure that the trail would cool, and he would be in the clear.

He was surprised when he went to Big Boys Bar and Grill and got into line dancing. He met a lady about his age that he enjoyed dancing with and soon the two of them were making the rounds of the clubs and not only line dancing but also enjoying conga and tango dancing. It turned out she was a dance instructor and soon she had him feeling comfortable trying any dance.

He knew better than allow his relationship to interfere with business and he slowed things down. He was disappointed when she let him know that she was moving on. He knew that was actually the right thing and he used his new dance skills to wine and dine women that were willing to engage in one-night stands.

He spent less time watching the dissection process and more time on optimizing the business. Having a full-time surgeon that was willing to work all seven days of the week let him think about expanding the business. He put out the word to his bosses and received congratulation for improving the business.

He was asked to first help set up a West Coast operation and then consider doing the same for the European, Russian, and Asian arenas. This was very attractive to him because it let him travel and see more of the world then just one city.

He promoted Luca into the role of manager of the Cleveland Operation.

He began to study the West Coast to understand the various communities to determine where an operation would best fit.

Los Angelos and San Francisco seemed to surface as the best location where harvesting would be the easiest. There seemed to be an endless supply of homeless people that would provide the raw materials, and the distributions network highway would provide coverage along the west coast and into the larger towns lying eastward.

He decided to travel to the two cities and get a firsthand look at the situation.

He had made his travel plans when he received word that the Cincinnati investigation was on the verge of solving the case.

He decided that instead of a trip west he would first take a trip to Cincinnati and get a firsthand look there.

He drove down and took a room at a Best Western at the north end of the 275-highway loop.

He took an Uber downtown to meet with his informant. They took a walk around the downtown and then had lunch down by the river front.

The news was that the body parts of a surgical nurse and the body parts of her surgeon fiancé had been identified. Additionally, a local surgeon was in custody and apparently

co-operating with authorities.

He contacted a local mafia operative and asked him whether the surgeon could have a fatal car accident or fall out of a balcony during a party or meet with some other fatal accident.

The answer was "Yes" for the right price. The right price turned out to be one hundred thousand dollars.

Reston was actually relieved about the cost and said he would leave the type of accident up to the operative.

He decided that he would return to Cleveland and wait to see how the elimination of the surgeon took place.

A week later he learned that the surgeon had taken an evening walk and had stepped in front of a bus and been killed.

He sent the second part of the money as he had promised to do.

He felt a sense of relief and once again focused his energy on getting the West Coast operation set up.

10 The Surgeon

*A*lex was glad to get out of the hospital. Her back ached where the bullet had been removed but it was the graze wound that was the most sensitive. A large pad had been put over it. She planned to keep it in place as long as possible. One of the nurses had fashioned a cover that could be used in the shower to keep the area dry while it healed.

Matt was there to drive her home, but she asked him to drop her off at the station because she wanted to get back to the case.

Matt shook his head but knew it was useless to argue. He knew she would be restless and bored in the apartment.

Alex walked into the bullpen area and realized that the team was in the huddle room. She got her usual cup of coffee and went in.

The bull pen area went silent as she crossed to the huddle room. She waved and said that there was nothing to see, and they should get back to work. She then went into the huddle room.

Trey was sitting back and talking to the team. Johnnie was working the keyboard of his computer. Bill and Trevor were both on the phone.

The room went silent as they all looked at Alex.

Alex smiled put her hand in front of her and said, "still black, not a ghost, why is everyone staring."

The huddle room door opened behind her, and the Chief walked in and asked what she was doing being at work.

Alex shook her head and said that she wanted to make sure the team got the bastard that had someone try to shoot her in the back.

Trey commented that he and Johnnie were hot on the trail and had determined the identity of a second surgeon that was most likely involved. He commented that Dr. Rogers had found a fingerprint on one of the legs. Johnnie ran the fingerprint through and had the name and address of a surgeon. We are about to go out and bring him in for questioning.

Alex nodded and said that talking to this surgeon might give them a break in the case. She added that they needed to make sure that he understood the consequences of not cooperating.

The Chief thanked Alex for coming in but said that she should take it easy and let the rest of the team do all the hard work. He turned to go back to his office.

Travis said he was disappointed that the big Boss had not sent the other boss home.

Alex smiled and pointed at Travis and said that as soon as she thought of the worst job on the case she would be sure to get him assigned to it.

The Chief shook his head and said that it sounded like the team was once again functioning as normal.

Alex smiled and blew a kiss at Trevor. She had to agree with the Chief, it felt like she was back in the groove.

Trey said that the surgeon in question was at the hospital, and they could go and bring him in for questioning.

Alex nodded and said that if he drove, she would go with him. She looked at Johnnie and asked him if that was OK with him.

Johnnie smiled and said that it was and that he would continue to identity the body parts that Dr. Rogers had processed.

Once in the car, Alex thanked Trey for having kept the investigation on track.

Trey thanked her and said it was easy because all of the guys wanted to make sure that we solved the case and nailed the guy that would have someone shoot you in the back. If there is a shootout, I want to be doing the shooting.

Alex remembered how she had reacted when Trey had been victimized and almost beaten to death. She had shot and killed four of the perpetrators and had shot the fifth one to get him to tell her who the boss of the operation was. She had no remorse and in the end she nailed the boss doing the ordering.

She nodded and said she understood the feeling and would step aside and give him the first shots.

They arrived at the hospital and inquired where they might find the doctor.

They went to the nurses station on the floor where they had been sent and asked for the doctor.

They watched him come down the hallway. It seemed he hesitated but then continued coming toward them.

He introduced himself as Dr. Leyton Riley. He then said that he recognized Alex and figured he was being approached about his moonlighting that he had briefly done.

Alex nodded and introduced Trey as her partner and that the two of them were there to interview him and to learn what they could about the moonlight operation. She asked if he was willing to come down to the station with them.

He asked if he was under arrest.

Alex smiled and replied that as long as he willing came along, no arrest was necessary.

He nodded and walked back to the nurses station and checked out for the rest of the day.

As they walked out, Alex suggested that they go and have lunch where they could have their discussion in a more pleasant environment.

Dr. Riley said that would be great and again thanked Alex for getting him out of the hospital in such a low-key manner.

Alex replied that she had no intention of being too public about the case and hoped that he would willing cooperate.

Dr. Riley asked if the body parts business was a legal one as he had been told it was.

Alex shook her head and said that it appeared that it was not a legal operation.

Dr. Riley said that he was shown a license that had a state seal on it and thought it legal, but he later suspected that it might not be.

Alex said that she had obtained the paperwork for the operation that was on file and on investigation the signature of the State Auditor had been found to be forged.

Dr. Riley asked if that made his actions illegal and was his medical licenses in jeopardy.

Alex replied that she had no desire to ruin his life, but she needed his cooperation to arrest the guy that was running such an operation.

She led the way into lunch and was greeted by the proprietor who welcomed her and smiled when she said she would take her usual table.

The proprietor nodded and took three menus to the table where Alex had shot and killed the huge brute that had come to shoot Johnnie.

The proprietor asked if he should expect any action.

Alex shook her head and said that everything would remain calm.

The proprietor smiled and said that the last advertisement that he had made that featured her had his lunch and dinner number up some thirty percent.

Alex said that she was glad and hoped it would stay up.

Dr. Riley asked if Alex was in business with the restaurant.

Alex shook her head and told him that she had shot and killed an attacker from the table that they were seated and since then she had made several advertisements for the restaurant. It seemed that macabre curiosity attracted diners and the business benefited by those curious to dine in the area where the action had taken place.

Dr. Riley shared that he had followed many of the news reports about her cases and was fascinated by the fact that she seemed to survive the gun battles she had been in.

He asked her if the current case would have any gun battles in it.

Alex said that if he was seen as a threat he would most likely be terminated. She shared the fact that this was her first day out of the hospital after being shot in the back by one of the persons associated with the body parts operation.

Dr. Riley frowned and asked if she thought that he was in imminent danger.

Alex replied that she thought that he indeed was in imminent danger.

Dr. Riley said that he was very willing to cooperate with Alex, but he did not have much information. He had only done two operating sessions when a fire had occurred.

The waiter came for the order, and they took a minute to put that in.

Then Alex explained that she thought that he could act as a decoy to attract the person sent to kill him. She wanted to capture that person alive so that her team could track who would have hired him. She wanted the location of the person who had run the body parts business.

Dr. Riley asked whether he had a choice.

Trey spoke up and said that the choice was between having protection or being alone when the killer sought him out.

"Ouch," Dr. Riley said. He shook his head and added that it was worse than being between a rock and a hard place.

Alex said she agreed and that she would see how he could appear to die so that the threat could be removed until the case was solved.

Dr. Riley asked what he would be doing while he was dead.

Trey suggested a vacation to some remote area.

Lunch was brought to the table and the three began to eat.

Alex suggested going to the station afterwards so that anyone watching them would see the Dr. being taken in.

Dr. Riley looked at her and asked if she was serious.

She replied that she was almost ninety per cent sure that they were being watched and that his presence with her was his death sentence.

Dr. Riley again shook his head and commented that she did not pull punches.

Trey smiled and said that working with Alex required that the punches were thrown otherwise you would get hit by a swarm of bullets.

The doctor smiled and asked if he had time for desert.

Alex nodded and said that was one thing there was always time for.

Trey drove to the station and Alex asked the Dr. to wear handcuffs into the station so that it appeared he was under arrest.

Once in the station Alex removed the handcuffs and led the way to the Chief's office.

She introduced the Chief to Dr. Riley and then explained that Dr. Riley had agreed to help in solving the body parts case.

The Chief asked how the Dr. would help.

Alex said that he had agreed to die.

The Chief gave a laugh and said that he knew that she had more in mind than killing a potential witness.

Dr. Riley said that he hoped so.

Alex said that she would like to take Dr. Riley to the morgue to work with Dr. Rogers. She wanted to identify the body parts that Dr. Riley had prepared.

After that she needed the doctor given police protection because she anticipated that the person who had run the body parts business would try to have the doctor killed.

The Chief asked who he should assign to protection duty.

Alex suggested that her team become his protection, but she and Trey would stay in the shadows because they had been on too many news casts.

The Chief nodded and said he trusted that she would set up the right protection duty.

Alex thanked him and suggested they go down to the morgue where all the body parts were currently located. She led the way and made the introductions.

Dr. Rogers immediately took over and asked if Dr. Riley would be able to identify the body parts that he was responsible for.

Dr. Riley replied that would be no problem.

Alex asked that when the two of them were through that she be called, and she would set up the surveillance coverage.

Once back in the huddle room she asked Trey to share that the two of them had done since they had left.

He surfaced the need to provide protection for the doctor and that the three of them had been volunteered to provide it.

Trevor laughed and said he would apologize for his earlier insult if that would relieve him of protection duty and asked why Trey got off so easy.

Bill said that he shouldn't suffer because he had a rude partner.

Johnnie said that next time he would check around the corner for shooters.

Alex shook her head and said that it was too late for all of them and let them know that her partner got special treatment.

She took in how good it felt to be back and interacting with the team. She knew that she had been right in coming in to work.

It was only a short time later when Dr. Rogers and Dr. Riley knocked on the huddle room door. Dr. Rogers said that he wanted Alex to know how helpful Dr. Riley had been and how shocked Dr. Riley had been when he found out that one of the first bodies he had dissected was that of a doctor who had been doing the same thing that he had had done.

Dr. Riley said that he was much more inclined to help in capturing this guy that had claimed to be running a legitimate business but had the previous Dr. and his fiancé killed.

Alex pointed at a chair and commented that if that didn't convince him of the jeopardy he was in then nothing could.

Dr. Riley sat down and asked what was to happened next.

Dr. Rogers excused himself and said he was going back to the morgue.

Alex said that she wanted to know where he lived and about his house or apartment. She added that she wanted the doctor to tell the team in detail what he did each workday and also what he did on weekends.

The doctor was silent for a moment then he began by describing where he lived.

He said that he lived in a second floor two-bedroom apartment on Burnett Avenue about three blocks from the hospital.

His life was rather dull and the routine he followed was to get up around six, have a quick coffee and muffin and then go out for a run for several blocks. He would return to his apartment take a quick shower and then walk to the hospital. He then spent the day at the hospital and usually would stop at one of the fast-food places to get a takeout and go back to his apartment and watch the evening news while he had his dinner.

Alex asked if anyone had any questions. The room was quiet. She then asked if he owned a car.

Dr. Riley said that he did not. He always took a cab or one of the other publicly available rides.

Alex asked what the most dangerous street crossing that he had to face each morning.

The doctor said that the Martin Luther King and Burnet corner was always the one that seemed the most dangerous.

Trey commented that he had driven by there several times when going to the VA facility and he agreed that particular crossing seemed to be the one that was one of the more dangerous places.

He figured it would be the best places to push someone in front of a bus.

Dr. Riley asked how they would be able to keep that from happening.

Alex pointed to Bill, Trevor and Johnnie and said that one of the three would be sitting at the corner dressed as a homeless outcast waiting for him each of the next few mornings until they caught the person that was going to push him in front of a moving bus. She said that she figured the person sent to kill him would be waiting to have a bus moving along at speed coming into the intersection to push him in front of.

Dr. Riley shook his head and said that being a decoy was becoming a little scary.

Alex said that it was, but the alternative choice left him totally unguarded. She made the point that he had a very poor alternative.

She added that she would have a police car parked at the apartment with observation duty to make sure that no one came to just shoot him while he was in his apartment.

Dr. Riley asked if she had any other kill scenarios in mind.

Alex gave a little laugh and said she could think of several others, but they entailed a much more elaborate approach that she did not think the killer would be able to carry out.

She said that she and Trey would be in the comfort of the hospital cafeteria and stay there throughout the day until they captured the killer.

Trevor shook his head and said that being on her team meant smelling like a homeless person, sitting out in the sun while she was comfortably sipping on coffee and eating a sweet roll.

Alex smiled and said that she was looking forward to his glorious morning in the sun.

11 The Break

Johnnie let everyone know that he was going to play his ukulele and put out his hat and collect donations as he sat on the corner pretending to be a beggar. He asked Alex to make sure the department knew that she was setting up a decoy at the corner so he would not get arrested.

Trevor said that he would bring his old tuba and do something similar, but he would use an old shoe to collect donations.

Alex laughed and suggested that he leave his tuba at home because she was sure he could not play it quiet enough to keep from getting a huge number of complaints.

Bob smiled and said he had considered bringing his accordion, but he doubted he could still play it.

Johnnie then said that he would split his take among the three of them and they might all be able to buy one cup of coffee to share.

Dr. Riley commented that their banter scared him. He wanted to make sure that they would have their eye out for his killer.

Alex smiled and agree that the three of them always scared her, but they always came through. She made the point that his killer would actually be easy to catch but they had to catch him just before he pushed him in front of the bus. She made the point that if the same person showed up two times in a row they would arrest him and bring him in for questioning. If he was the one then there needed to be a news release showing the doctor in front of the bus with blood running down the street.

She said that she would work with the Metro leadership to set up that scene and with the department film crew to get it filmed.

Dr. Riley said that sounded very elaborate. He asked when that would take place.

Alex suggested that evening and she would have the person editing it put in the early morning sun into the picture.

Dr. Riley nodded and said that things seemed to be moving along at a fast pace.

Trey replied that it was either fast or slow in the detective business and that a moderate pace was not known.

Alex made a call and explained to the person at the other end that she needed the help of the Metro in solving the case she was working. After reaching the President she explained what she needed. He said he would make a call and have one of the spare busses ready for the filming. After that they agreed on the location.

Alex called the police film department and arranged for someone to shoot the scene. She asked that some fake blood be brought to the scene.

She then asked Dr. Riley if he was ready to die.

He smiled and said that he was ready if it was just fake.

A few moments later a person knocked at the door and said that the camera crew was ready to go.

Alex stood up and asked who wanted to go and direct the movie scene.

Everyone stood up and followed. Bob and Trevor got into the camera van and the rest got into Alex's car. Trey was behind the wheel and asked where they were going.

Alex gave him the address, and they all left. She had picked out a street that went downhill like the one on Martin Luther King Drive where she expected the attempted killing to take place.

The camera crew set up, and the Metro bus driver positioned the bus as instructed. The camera man asked the doctor to lay face down in the street with his left ear to the street and his arms splayed out. His sports jacket was to be open. His mouth needed to be slightly open so that the blood looked like it was coming out from both his mouth and his head.

He then pulled one of the doctor's shoes off and tossed it down just below the pool of blood.

He asked the bus driver to look astonished or have a disbelieving look on his face.

Alex looked at the scene and commented that she wished she had thought about asking for some extra people to be onlookers.

The camera man said that he could make that happen and asked his two helpers to put on their more casual outfits on. He then set up the camera on a timer and positioned everyone and pushed the remote he had in his hand and took his first shot. He set up several scenes and took shots of each from several angles.

Alex was not sure which scene was best, but she liked the one that had a police officer checking for a pulse best.

She thanked everyone and asked who wanted to be treated to Johnnie's favorite place to eat.

The filming crew asked if they were invited. And the bus driver did the same.

Alex nodded and said the treat was on her. She asked Johnnie were he wanted to go. He suggested where the logs could be seen floating down the river. Alex knew which restaurant that was and gave them a call and asked for reservations for nine.

Dr. Riley asked if they would all allow him to pay.

Alex smiled and thanked him for the offer but said it would look awkward if later they had to arrest him. She said she would have to decline but if Trevor wanted to step up she would be glad to let him pay.

Trevor shook his head and said that he had just spent the last of his saving to pay his son's college tuition to Harvard.

Everyone on the team laughed since they knew that his son was president of his own company and had been out of college for at least ten years and had not attended Harvard.

Alex nodded and said that then it was settled, and they should all head to the restaurant and watch the logs float by, and Johnnie could tell them about having learned to play the ukelele and she would pay.

During dinner Dr. Riley asked if he could let his family know that he would really not be dead.

Alex replied that he could, but he would need to make sure his family did not share it with anyone and after the news announcing his death they would put out a statement that they would like to be given the space to mourn.

Dinner ended and the team decided to go their separate ways.

Alex had Trey drop Johnnie and her at the apartment. The crime scene tapes at the apartment were down but the yellow sketch marks on the sidewalk and on the street were still visible. The outline of the bikes made her think about the fact that they would need to walk to work unless they got their bikes back. She asked if Johnnie wanted to come with her to her favorite bike shop to see if they could replace their bikes.

Johnnie asked why he couldn't just get his from the station.

Alex replied that it would most likely be months before they got their bikes back and she knew for sure she would need to have hers go through a major overhaul. She added that they could probably get a good deal if the shop had any good used bikes.

Johnnie said that it would be fun to shop for a new bike and asked when she thought they could get to the shop.

Alex replied that it would be right after he got off his first day of killer patrol.

Johnnie shook his head and said, "wow yes that begins in the morning. A better question is how will I get in place at the corner."

Alex said that Trey would pick them up at six in the morning and by seven he would be on station. She and Trey would park nearby until it was time for the Dr. to get to the corner.

Once the Dr. made it to the hospital the three of them would return to the station review the death scenes and pick their favorite for release to the news.

Johnnie said it sounded like a good plan.

Alex said good night and took the elevator to the top floor and walked down toward her apartment. She was surprised to see Sandra sitting on a chair in front of her apartment.

Sandra greeted her and said that the Chief had asked her if she was willing to be one of the guards that he was posting. She and her husband had volunteered to be on coverage duty. She said that there was a third volunteer who said he had been the guard outside of Trey's room when he was in the VA hospital.

Alex thanked her and asked whether a glass of milk and some cookies would help.

Sandra smiled and said that she was hoping for just such an offer.

When Alex walked into the apartment she was surprised to see Matt sitting on the couch reading.

He said that his boss told him to take one more day off and make sure that she got a good night's sleep.

Alex smiled and said she had no doubt about being ready for a good night's sleep but wondered if she would be able to do so with the bandages that she had on.

Matt said he would look at the bandages and see if he could make them less bulky so that she could be comfortable in bed.

She gave him a kiss and then said she had to deliver some milk and cookies to her guard at the door and then she would be ready for him to see about making her bandages less bulky.

Trey let her know that he would be leaving about five in the morning. His team was swinging by to pick him up.

Alex said that would work for her because she and Johnnie would be picked up by Trey a few minutes later. She shared that Johnnie had promised her a pancake breakfast with two poached eggs on the pancakes.

Matt smiled and said that his team was arriving with a breakfast sandwich and coffee for him.

Alex said that made the coming morning convenient for both of them.

The next morning Trey showed up, and Bill and Trevor were following in their car. Trevor said that Bill had not let him buy donuts and insisted they would follow and make sure that things went down as expected.

Alex thanked them for coming along. She said they should all get on the same chat group so they could communicate with each other at the scene.

Trey then led the way to the corner were they expected the attempted killing to take place.

Alex watched as Johnnie walked to the corner and sat down and placed his hat at his feet. She had asked Bill and Travis to park a few cars behind them. She adjusted her mirror so she could see the Dr. approaching the corner.

She looked along the sidewalk and saw no one but the doctor approaching the corner. Then a person stepped out from between two of the houses and began following the doctor.

She said that she thought the pusher was now behind the doctor.

She heard Johnnie asking for money for breakfast.

The doctor ignored him, but she was surprised to see the pusher take a roll of money from is pocket and put a bill into Johnnie's hat.

The walk light turned green, and the doctor walked across. The pusher turned to his right and walked down the sidewalk.

Alex told the doctor to go to work and for Johnnie to walk across the street and come back to the car and they would all go back to the station.

Once back at the station Bill suggested that they should arrange for a bus to come by at the right time.

Alex agreed and said she would arrange it for the coming morning.

Johnnie said that he had taken a picture of the suspected killer and would see if he could identify who that person was.

The film crew leader came in with his computer and said that he had several options to pick from that could be used as a news announcement.

Alex asked Johnnie to help get the computer hooked to the large screen. She was pleased that all the scenes seemed real. She said she thought the best one was with a police officer checking out the doctor to see if he was dead.

The entire team agreed. The film crew leader said that he liked that one as well and that he would put more people into the scene and arrange for its release when Alex gave him the order.

Alex thanked him and after he had left she said she was going shopping for a bike.

She then let the team know that Johnnie would be the person at the corner on the following morning and if the same guy showed up they would take him into custody and check him out. She made the point that if either Bill or Trevor were to be at that corner they would likely spook the potential killer.

Trevor whined and said that he had wasted the entire previous evening polishing his tuba so that he could play his part.

Alex shook her head and told him that he should then take it to his high school and donated it to the band.

Trey said that he would stay with Bill and Trevor to see if they could figure out who had set fire to the warehouse.

Alex asked Johnnie to drive to the bike shop.

Once there she was greeted by her name as she walked in. She liked the fact that the owner was always polite and cordial. She asked if he had any specials on some high-end bikes.

He asked whether she wanted brand new or was she interested in some good used ones.

Alex replied that a bargain in a good used one would be nice.

He showed her one that had a belt drive that he was offering at half the price of a new one.

Alex liked it immediately and asked if a carrier rack could be put on the back. She asked to take if for a ride around the lot. She came back and let him know that she would take it.

She then pointed to Johnnie and said he needed a bargain too.

The shop owner pointed to a bike that had a sign advertising it as a limited-edition Amsterdam bike that was also belt driven. It was a little less expensive but did not have as big a discount as the one she had chosen.

Johnnie said that he liked the blue color and the front trey that it had and asked if he could take a quick spin.

When he finished he said that he would take it.

Alex took the bike rack out from the trunk and set it up. She and Johnnie wheeled their bikes out and put them in the rack. Her bike was white and his was a lustrous blue. She commented that they looked great.

Johnnie agreed and said they should celebrate getting new bikes.

Alex agreed and asked what he had in mind.

Johnnie suggested a picnic on the weekend along the Loveland bike trail.

Alex said that sounded great and she should be healed enough to enjoy the ride.

They left the car in the police lot in its normal parking spot so that Trey could find it the next morning.

Alex led off and the two rode their new bikes back to the apartment.

Sandra saw Alex pushing her bike up the hall and let out a whistle and commented that her new bike was a beauty.

Alex chuckled and said that the compliment would get Sandra an extra cookie and that today it would be warm because she was baking a new batch of oatmeal raisin cookies.

She went into the apartment and put her new bike in the rack where her old bike was usually placed. It was then she remembered leaving her new rack in the trunk of the car.

The next morning when Trey picked them up Johnnie volunteered to take both his and her bike rack and put them in his apartment.

Alex thanked him.

As they were driving to where Johnnie would be sitting she told him that if the same guy showed up that he should arrest him.

Johnnie said it would be no problem.

Alex pointed out Bill and Trevor's car as they approached. They paused for a moment to let Johnnie out and then drove on and parked a short distance from the corner. Alex checked out the teams connection and was pleased that everyone including the doctor was on.

It seemed like a repeat of the morning before but this time the bus that Alex had arranged would make its approach and the would-be killer would be apprehended as he was about to push the doctor out in front of it.

Alex watched the scene unfold as if it had been rehearsed. The bus was starting across the intersection, the perpetrator stepped forward to push the doctor and as he placed his hand on the doctors back, Johnnie put the point of his revolver to the pushers head and said that he was under arrest and to step back.

Both Bill and Travis rushed up and put the perpetrator in hand cuffs, read him his rights, and led him back toward their car.

Alex got out and walked up to the doctor and told him to go to the hotel in Blue Ash and enjoy the next week or so until the case could be resolved. She said that the news release would be in the morning reporting and would most likely make all the channels.

12 Order Fulfilment

Reston was relieved when he watched the morning news. The report focused on the death of Dr. Leyton Riley. It showed the doctor splayed out in the street with blood running out of his head. Things seemed to be looking up. He had been able to fulfill eighty percent of the orders that he had brought with him from the Cincinnati operation with new body parts garnered in his new location. His bosses were pleased, and he was on the road to focusing on the expansion of the business to the west coast, Asia, and Europe.

He was fairly certain that the case would go cold at the Cincinnati end.

He felt very good about how his new crew operated. They were much better at bringing in the people he identified, and they were very good at making sure the personal possessions such as the vehicles or bicycles were disposed of in an effective manner.

He had arranged for the cars to be sold and sent out of state, and he liked the fact that his workers filed off any serial numbers, painted the bikes, and sold them to a local bike shop. He let them keep the money they made from that endeavor.

He felt that things couldn't be going much better.

He had also learned about a new technique to get rid of the unused body parts that was referred to as liquification. This provided a way to process those parts and did not require the use of the oven. It eliminated any smoke or odor associated with that process. He studied the process and decided on getting a model designed for large pets. The model was large enough for his needs and it kept the seller from linking his operation with human bodies. He got good feedback about how well it worked from his two workers. They commented that all the waste was an odorless white powder.

Things were going well enough and smoothly enough that he gave his three workers a significant bonus for their good work.

Had he known what was happening in Cincinnati he would have arranged for a new hiding place versus setting up travel arrangements.

Back in Cincinnati, the person hired to push the doctor in front of the bus was sitting in a cell.

Alex and the team were sitting in the Chief's office updating him on the situation. Alex highlighted the fact that they had arrested the potential killer as he was about to push the doctor in front of the bus and the fact that the doctors, "death" was making the morning's news. She shared that the doctor was planning to take a fishing trip to the Tetons for the next several weeks or until he got word he could come back to life.

She had questioned the perp and had learned he was to earn five thousand dollars for pushing the doctor. He was a legal immigrant that did small jobs for a local drug dealer. She said they would need to spend more time with him to see if he could identify someone that was connected with the human body parts business.

She turned to Bill and Travis and asked them to update the Chief on how they were doing on finding out who had set the fire.

Bill said that they figured that the fire had been set by the person hired to clean the facility. They had been waiting to get Johnnies help in zeroing in on who the cleaning person might be. They had a list of people offering that service and need to somehow narrow the list down so they could get in the field and question these cleaners.

Alex suggested they look for any cleaners doing advertising in the help pages versus the larger operations. She figured that it would be an individual that was on their own.

Johnnie said he would be glad to get on it immediately.

The Chief thanked them for the update and said that Dr. Rogers had finished processing all the body parts and had put all the reports online.

Alex suggested they go to the huddle room and get organized. She wanted to make some sort of breakthrough that led to the location of the person who had set up the operation in Cincinnati because she was fairly sure he would be setting up a similar operation somewhere nearby.

Johnnie reminded the team that he had already done an initial search of the most probable cities. Three were in Ohio, one in Indiana, one in Pennsylvania and one in New York.

Alex said she was betting on Ohio, but she would go wherever Johnnie pointed. She asked him what his search parameters were. He said that he would look for buildings or houses that had sold since the fire. He hoped that it was not too lengthy of a list, but he figured he had ways of speeding up the search.

Alex asked him to focus on getting her a list of potential new sites before focusing on who set the local fire.

Travis gave a moan and said that once again he was being put on the back burner and that he would be happy to bring in an extra bear claw for her to enjoy so that he could get equal treatment.

The Chief shook his head and told the team to work out their problems outside of his office or he would assign them all to ground clean up duty.

Bill put his arm over Travis's shoulder and as he led him out of the office he said that he felt his pain.

Alex smiled saluted the Chief and said that everything was good.

Once in the huddle room she asked if Bill and Trevor would question the perp they had locked up and see if they could get some sort of information that would help in determining who had set up the hit and where the kill order came from. She added that some names and locations would be useful. They badly needed to find the new location because she was sure that harvesting of human body parts was profitable enough that it was the drug war equivalent that they now faced.

Bill and Travis left the huddle room and said that they would be back before lunch. Travis smiled and said that he was going to let Bill be the good cop and he was going to be the bad one.

Alex smiled and said that they would both be playing their natural role.

Bill nodded and added that he agree wholeheartedly with her.

Alex turned her attention back to Johnnie and suggested they focus first on the three locations in Ohio.

Trey suggested starting with the most industrial area and the area with the most homeless people.

Johnnie ran that and got the order of the cities with the highest populations and the highest homeless people. He put them up on the screen in one two three order. They were Cleveland, Columbus, and Cincinnati.

Trey said that he would definitely start with Cleveland because it also had a sprawling population down towards Akron.

Johnnie said he would tap into the latest filings of sales registered in the courthouse.

There was only one warehouse that had changed hands and that was between two large freight companies. There was a large number of homes but only about a dozen of larger homes.

Alex suggested they take a look at the larger homes and decide by location and by the arial look which ones they felt were the most likely.

It did not take long before they had shortened the list to the three most likely.

They used the internet and several realty services to look over the three.

Alex picked the two most likely and then said that it was time for the team to take a road trip.

Johnny volunteered to get the team a nice conversion van or something like it so they could all drive up together.

Trey volunteered to make reservations at an Embassy suites.

Alex called Trevor and asked how they were doing with getting information.

He responded that they were sitting at his desk having their perp looking through pictures to see who he could identify associated with his order to push the doctor in front of the bus.

He picked out the three dead shooters and Reston Sanclemente who was the person he saw with his boss.

It turns out his boss has a warrant out for not having paid over twelve speeding tickets so we will be able to pick him up to get more information.

Alex said they should put their perp back in the holding cell and get together for a team road trip discussion.

A short time later, Bill and Trevor came into the team room and asked where they were going.

Trey explained that they had narrowed their guess as to where the new body part processing operation had relocated to two places in Cleveland.

He pointed at Alex and said she was ready to leave and see if they could find the new operation and close it down.

Bill commented that would be great, but what were the chances that one of the two places was the new operation site.

Alex replied that Trey and Johnnie had picked the city together. Then Johnnie had identified the sales that were registered since the fire closed the operation in Cincy and then they had worked together and narrowed it to two places. She said that only footwork would now resolve the situation.

Trevor nodded and said that so far Johnnie was batting a thousand and he was ready to get the footwork done.

Alex said she was going to clear the trip with the Boss and that they should all plan on meeting in the station parking lot early in the morning and they would drive to Cleveland and check out the two places.

The Chief listened to Alex's request to take a field trip to Cleveland. He said he supported the trip and that he would call the Cleveland Chief of Police in to let him know that the five of them would be up.

Alex thanked him and suggested that if they found the operation they would get the local police involved in shutting down the operation. She pointed out that they might need to get a speedy search warrant so they could enter the operation.

The Chief agreed and said he would put in the call as soon as she left.

Alex thanked him and said that she planned to leave early the next day but would stay in contact as they drove up to Cleveland.

Early the next morning the stars were still twinkling in the sky as Alex and the team got into their Mercedes luxury van that Johnnie had rented from his car rental friend at a great price

Meanwhile in Cleveland Reston was driving to the Cleveland airport to get on a flight to Los Angelos. He was going out to meet with the local mafia head to see about setting up a body parts operation. He had no idea how close he was to being shut down in Cleveland nor how detrimental the closure would be to his wellbeing.

Alex contacted the Chief and got the number to the Police Chief in Cleveland and after introduction and a rather lengthy discussion she got assurances that she would have search warrants for the two addresses and two police cars backing the team up at each locations. The Cleveland police would bring the warrants for each site with them.

She shared with the team that they would meet the Cleveland team at each site and then together they would surround the buildings and proceed to go in.

She reminded everyone to be ready but not to shoot unless they were shot at or saw someone about to shoot.

Trevor shook his head and said the case that had them coming down from the attic and walking into a hail of bullets was waking him up at nights. He hoped that the group they faced was less gun happy. He commented that he had his entire body Kevlar body suit with him.

Alex said that she was not expecting gunfire, but they should all wear their bullet proof vests and that if they had no vests they would be left in the van. She was pleased to hear everyone say they had brought theirs along.

They arrived at the first house at eleven and were met their by the two Cleveland Patrol cars.

Alex made sure the correctness of the paperwork and of the address. The house looked as isolated as it had looked from the Google Maps view, but it was clear that whoever lived there was taking great care of the place and the flowers around the perimeter of the house and the thriving back garden reduced the likelihood that this was a body process site to nearly zero.

Alex asked everyone to stay back but asked Bill and Trevor to step far enough into the yard to be able make sure no one left by the back door.

She and Trey walked up the steps and walked slowly along the porch and rang the doorbell. Trey took the front and was greeted by an elderly gentleman who asked what he was selling. Trey showed his badge, gave a brief explanation, and asked if he and his partner could come in.

The door opened wider, and an elderly gentleman stepped out and saw the two police cars and the black van. He commented that it seemed that they had expected trouble.

Alex replied that they were pleased to not have any and wondered if they could get a quick look inside.

The wife came to the door and said that they should come in and reassure themselves that whatever they were looking for in the house they would find only the old furniture and things that she and her husband had accumulated for over the past fifty years. They had just moved in during the spring and where still trying to get their things unpacked.

Alex followed her in, and Trey and the husband came in. Alex thanked the wife for the offer of coffee or tea but the two of them had another address to check out. She apologized for disturbing them.

The wife said that no apology was necessary, and they should be careful at the next place.

Alex nodded and said she would be very careful there.

She went out to the two police cars and spent a few minutes talking to the four officers. She introduced everyone and then asked if they knew a good lunch place and added that the Cincinnati detective unit would pay for lunch.

Lunch was at a Mexican restaurant that had a lunch special for only twelve dollars a plate. There was a wide variety of lunch plates that went from twelve to twenty dollars. Everyone selected a different item.

Alex selected Polynesian Pork tacos and an order of onion straws for the table. Trey ordered West coast shrimp tacos and Johnnie ordered smoked brisket tacos. Bill and Trevor both ordered Nashville Hot chicken tacos. They all knew that everyone would be trying a little of everyone else's orders.

The four police officers were sitting at tables at each end of the long table that the five members of the Cincinnati team was sitting.

One of them asked how long the five of them had worked together.

Trevor laughed and said that it had been a lifetime, and they were all still talking to each other.

The lunch took over an hour and after everyone had finished they got up and walked out to their cars.

Alex gave the next address and one of the Cleveland group commented that he knew the neighborhood and it was not as nice as the one they had just left. He figured that this time they should all take positions around the house.

The two police cars led the way.

Alex asked everyone to put on their Kevlar jackets and check their weapons. She commented that she had a bad feeling about the next address.

As they drove into the neighborhood she became almost certain that they were at the new human processing center. She let the team know that she was having one of her Déjà vu moments.

Trevor nodded and said that he was then sure they were at the new human body parts processing center.

Alex asked the four police officers to put on their body armor.

One of the officers asked what made her think there would be shooting.

Alex shook her head and said that she was not sure, but it was better to be safe.

Bob and Trevor took the back of the house. She and Trey took the front.

She asked the four policemen to take the sides. She looked at Johnnie and told him to go wherever he liked but to keep his head down.

She walked up to the front door and announced that the house was surrounded and anyone inside should come out with their hands up.

A few seconds afterwards there was a shot fired from a second story window and one of the police officers went down.

Alex watched as Johnnie rushed over to the officer and as he knelt in front of him he pointed his gun up at some target and fired three times. A moment later she heard what she was sure was a body hit the ground.

She knew that whomever it was would be dead.

She heard Bill shout out telling someone to stop and that they were under arrest and then several gunshots.

Then she could hear a third person shout out that he was surrendering and that he was coming out with his hands up.

She looked at her watch and realized that the entire episode had taken less than four minutes.

Trevor kicked in the front door and the two of them rushed in. Two police officers came in the back and the four of them checked out the entire place to make sure there was no one else.

Alex noted the cooler locker that was on the same level as what looked like a surgery room. She had no desire to look in.

Alex walked back outside as an EMT unit arrived. She walked over to where the downed officer was sitting. He had been hit in the chest area; his body shield had cracked but had held. The EMT team checked him out and Bill said that he had been shot as well and just wanted to have them take a quick look.

Alex walked over to him and asked to see where he had been hit. There was a flattened bullet on the Kevlar jacket. She gave him a hug and said that she hoped the bruise would not be too bad.

Neither of the two had anything worse than what would be a bruise the next day.

A swarm of police cars with their lights flashing arrived. The coroner and his team began processing the two dead shooters.

Alex watched as one of the officers that she was sure he would be the Police Chief approached.

He walked up to her and introduced himself and then smiled and said he had been warned about the Cincinnati Black Annie Oakley and asked which of the two she had shot.

Alex smiled and said that she had not fired her weapon, but Wild Bill Johnnie Hancock had shot and killed the shooter that had shot one of his officers and Wild Bill Danson had survived getting shot in the chest as he shot and killed the second.

She then suggested that the coroner not worry too much about processing the two dead shooters and that he go inside and begin to examine the body parts that he would find in the cooler on the first floor.

The Police Chief walked over to the coroner and after a moment came back and asked about the body parts. He asked how they would be identified.

Alex said that they were still in the process of identifying the body parts that had been in the cooler at the Cincinnati operation and that Dr. Rogers the coroner there would be a good person to contact, and she pointed at Johnnie and said that he would be the resource for one of the Cleveland IT guys. He was the one that was identifying most of the body parts. She added that the surgeon that was doing the work in Cleveland needed to be identified and arrested. He most probably believed he was working for a legitimate company, but he was most likely aware that something was not quite right. She suggested stationing a police squad at the house and that on Monday during the day or early evening they should expect the arrival of the surgeon. They should also expect the arrival of the person running the operation.

She followed the coroner into the house and led him to the cooler door. She said she preferred to remain outside of the cooler.

The coroner and his team went in but two of his team almost immediately came out and said that the scene was horrible, and they needed to get outside.

Alex said she had the same reaction, and she still had nightmares about it.

The Police Chief walked in and looked through the door and shook his head. He asked if the parts came from cadavers.

Alex shook her head. She said that the ones in Cincinnati had been linked with homeless people, and a few had been identified from missing person's reports. They were missing persons who had gone to work and not returned home that evening.

The Chief said that he was going to keep this as quiet as possible and that it would scare the entire region if it got out.

Alex agreed and pointed out that the organizer had not been on location and was somewhere around and needed to be apprehended.

"Damn" was the Chief's last words.

<u>13 Return</u>

Reston looked out the window and watched the horizon sink as the plane turned and got into the position to make a landing. It was the end to what he saw as a very successful and productive trip. He had made contact with the LA branch of the mafia and had started the process of getting the parts business established. He would return in a few weeks and help them take the next steps in getting the business going. He knew the details and timing to establish the harvesting, processing, and distribution network. The distribution system was the first thing that was needed then the harvesting network needed to be put in place. The processing entailed the brick-and-mortar elements and were actually the easiest to put in place.

The plane landed but it seemed to take forever to get to the gate and then to unload. He waited impatiently for his bag to slide down onto the rotating carrier. He got his bags and went out and had to stand in line to catch a cab.

During the ride to the house, he made a call to his bodyguard, but Luca did not answer. He called Angello and Dario and none of them answered.

Alarm bells went off in his head. He then saw a police car parked about a block from the house. He told the cab driver to keep going and that he wanted to go to a hotel. They drove past the house and then he asked the cab driver to turn and come back up on the next block. He asked the cab to wait for him while he checked to see if anyone was home at his friend's house. He then got out and slowly walked back to the house on the side that was out of view to the police car. He got to the alley way behind the house and opened the side door. He knew immediately something was wrong. He quietly went through the house. He carefully looked out the window and saw the yellow outline markings of a body on the gravel drive on that side of the house. He looked out the back and saw a similar outline near the garage. Both areas were taped off with yellow tape.

He opened his safe and took out the cash and put it in a large briefcase. He then closed the safe and took his briefcase.

He walked back out the side door and walked back to the cab and asked to be taken to the Sheraton.

He was in a stunned state. He wondered how the police had found his operation. The only thing that made sense was that the Cincinnati Detective group had somehow been able to trace him.

He knew that he was in trouble and that he would have to contact his leader that was in New York and get instructions in how to proceed.

Trey sat in the breakfast area waiting for his pancakes and eggs to get prepared. He was nursing his cup of coffee and had a piece of buttered toast with strawberry jam that he was nibbling on. He watched as Alex made her way to his table. She stopped and got a glass of orange juice and a cup of coffee and put in her request at the grill window.

Alex was not surprised to see Trey sitting at the table. The two of them seemed to trade morning breakfast arrivals. Once she had had her breakfast order in she went to the table and asked how his night had been.

Her phone rang just as she sat down. She answered and listened to the Police Chief as he told her that all three of the confiscated phones had received a call a few moments earlier. Alex thanked him for letting her know and suggested the call came from their boss. She asked if his police squad had seen anyone arrive at the house. The chief replied that the only action had been a taxi that drove by but did not stop at the house.

Alex thanked him for the call and let him know that the team would be in to interrogate the person that they had captured at the house.

Johnnie walked into the breakfast area carrying his computer and came over to the table. He said that he had continued to process the information about the current operation and had realized that the little house across the alley was owned by the same person that owned the house they had raided.

Alex asked what name was on both of the deeds.

Johnnie looked that up and said that a Preston Clemente was the person listed.

Alex smiled and said that their perp must like his name because he had added and deleted a few letters and had almost the same name. She asked Johnnie to check to see if someone of that name had checked into any hotel close to the houses.

She suggested he put in his breakfast order in before doing any more digging.

About the same time Bob and Trevor walked in and came over to the table.

She asked Bob how he was feeling.

Bob replied that he was fine but did have a hand sized bruise on his chest.

A few moments later Johnnie said he had three hits but none of the names were the one that they had discussed.

Alex asked where the hotels were located. She then asked Bill, Trevor, and Trey if they were willing to go to the hotels and show the desk personnel a picture of Reston to determine if he had checked into one of the three.

They all agreed to do so. Trevor asked what she would be up to.

Alex said that she was going to question the one person who had survived to learn what she could about the operation. She figured that Johnnie would be instrumental in checking out what they learned.

Johnnie was at the wheel as they arrived at the Central station. He drove to the entrance to the underground car park.

Alex showed her badge and the guard said he was expecting them. She handed him a bag of chocolate and told him to enjoy himself.

She led the way up the stairs and then checked in at a desk at the entrance to the building. She had been expected and was shown the way to the Chief's office.

He greeted her and Johnnie and asked if she would like a coffee or something else to drink.

Both she and Johnnie said coffee would be fine.

The Chief then said he was going to call a couple of the policemen in that had been with her the previous day because they wanted to say thanks.

Alex and Johnnie sat down and a few moments later the Chief returned with the two. One of them was the officer that had been shot.

He came over and shook Alex's hand and said that his wife insisted that he invite her over for dinner if she had time.

Alex smiled and said that the offer warmed her heart but that it was not necessary. Alex took out a bag of Godiva chocolates and said that he should give it to his wife.

She gave one to his partner and one to the Chief.

His partner commented that her insistence that they wear their protective gear had at first irritated them but as it turned out the situation warranted it and that in the future they would be more cautious.

Alex nodded. She related the fact that her team members had at first struggled with her insistence of wearing their Kevlar outfits but after a few shootouts they had all become believers.

She suggested that the Kevlar outfits made it less bulky and more comfortable to be protected and maybe the Cleveland Police could make it part of the official gear.

The Chief asked what Alex planned to do next.

She shared that her three other members were checking three hotels to see if they could apprehend the leader of the operation and that if one of them located this person she would like the Cleveland police to back her up and then make the arrest.

Both officers immediately spoke up that they and the other two who had been at the house would all volunteer to make the arrest.

The Chief said that he supported the four being the ones that would take the lead, but he would probably have some other units ready to respond as well. He said that he would like the arrest to take place without any shooting.

He also reiterated the fact that he did not want any word to get out on the type of operation that was going on.

Alex smiled and said he sounded just like her Chief, and she agreed with the sentiment. The fact that the mafia was getting into the body parts business scared the daylights out of her.

The Chief led the way down to the holding area and talked briefly to the sergeant that was in charge.

After the Chief left, the sergeant looked at her and asked what she had done for the Chief that had him giving her the green light to do whatever she wanted.

Alex smiled and handed the sergeant a bag of chocolate and said that a little sweetness always made things easier.

She said that he looked like he could scare a person if he felt like it and that she wanted the person that she was about to question to be scared. She asked if he would threaten the person, tell him that he would most likely get the gas chamber or spend the rest of his life in a top security prison where he would most likely be the girl.

The sergeant shook his head, smiled, and said that the chocolates did make it easier. He showed her to the room where the questioning was to take place and he explained that a monitor would be recording the session, and he took her to the monitoring room and introduced the monitor who it turned out was a new policewoman on her first assignment.

She and Johnnie were handed headsets and the policewoman explained how the system worked and then adjusted everything so that she would have a good recording.

Alex thanked her and handed her a bag of chocolate, and they went into the questioning room.

Johnnie asked her how many bags of candy she had left.

Alex smiled and asked what he had in mind.

Johnnie said that he wanted to be the kind, generous, good guy and be able to offer the perp a candy.

Alex nodded and asked whether she had to be the bad cop.

Johnnie shook his head and said that her just being herself would probably scare the perp.

There was a knock on the room door and then the hand cuffed perp was brought in and chained to a ring on the table.

Alex greeted him by name and introduced herself and Johnnie. She asked Dario to explain his role in the body parts business.

Dario's hands were shaking, and he had trouble answering her.

Alex asked why his hands were shaking.

Dario replied that he did not want to be put to death.

Alex asked if he had put anyone to death to get their body parts.

Dario shook his head in the negative but did not speak.

Johnnie pushed a chocolate to him and suggested he eat it and asked whether a bottle of water would help.

Dario said that a bottle of water would be nice.

Alex looked at Johnnie and told him that he shouldn't be so nice to a person that was probably a killer of innocent people.

There was a knock on the door, and an officer came in with three bottles of water.

Alex paused and took a long drink.

She then leaned in and put her face about a foot from Dario's and looked him in the eyes and asked if he had watched innocent people being killed.

Tears came into Dario's eyes, and he shook his head in the affirmative. He then whispered out the fact that Luca and Angelo were the ones who either shot or slit the person's throat. He said they made fun of him because he often had to go and throw up.

"So, you were queasy, but you went along," Alex asked.

Dario said that he didn't have a choice.

Alex slammed her hand on the table as if angry. And said that he was a person too weak to make a choice to save innocent people.

Johnnie quietly said that it was not appropriate for her to lose her temper.

Dario said that his entire family was part of the mafia, and he had no place to go if he were to quit. He would be ostracized but more likely he would be killed.

Tell me how many people you have so far participated in killing.

Dario was silent for a few moments and then said there were probably fourteen.

The number caught Alex by surprise, and she went silent. She had spotted the parts of someone that was either small or very young. It made her feel sick. She wished she would have been faster at stopping the operation.

Johnnie pushed another chocolate to Dario and asked what the age range was of the people he watched being killed.

Dario began to sob openly. He finally was able to say nine years old to forty-five.

Alex asked how the target people were identified.

Dario said that he was not sure of the details, but the boss had access to several participating doctors, and he also had access to the hospital databases.

Alex then asked the name of the doctor that did the dissections.

Dario said that he only knew him as Dr. Riley.

Alex let Dario know that the current questioning session was over and that his continued cooperation would make it likely that he could keep from getting a death penalty, but his involvement was deep, and she said he would most likely spent much of the rest of his life in prison.

Alex took the candy bag from Johnnie and gave it to Dario and said she was sure that there would be several more questioning sessions so that he could clarify in detail what had transpired at the house.

Two officers came in and took Dario out of the room.

Alex stood for a moment and asked Johnnie to give her a hug. She was surprised at how empty she felt. She knew that she and the team worked as fast as possible to catch the killers, but to have an operation that in the two months since the Cincinnati operation had been closed kill fourteen people including a child overwhelmed her.

The Chief walked in and said that he was overwhelmed by what he had heard and that in his entire thirty-five-year career he had not handled a case like this one.

Alex nodded and agreed that it was mind boggling, but she had just closed two cases that were horrible. One had a nationwide organization that killed almost two hundred women after abusing them and the other had one individual killing and burying her victims along the US, Canadian border.

The Chief shook his head and said that he didn't know how she could handle it.

Alex agreed and shared the fact that her team had both team and individual sessions with the department phycologist every month.

They also spent many weekends doing picnics and going on outings together.

She pointed at Johnnie and said he took them to the best restaurants for lunch and made sure she ended up paying.

She said that she would be scheduling several additional sessions with the phycologist as soon as she was back in Cincinnati because she knew this case was having a huge impact on her.

The Chief said that he would check to see when the phycologist in his department was available.

The policewoman in the booth asked if he would support her getting an appointment.

The Chief replied that he supported her.

He then shared that one of her members had called in to let the department know that the person they were looking for had checked in at the hotel where they were, and they were standing by to wait for backups.

Alex looked at the texts on her phone. She had Bill texting a no hit and Trey with a negative face and the red circle with a line through it. Trevor had an explosion emoji and simple said hit.

She asked if she could ride along to the hotel to be part of the arrest.

The Chief said she could ride in his car.

Alex stopped by the recording booth and asked that the recording be handled as evidence She told the policewoman to follow through on getting some counseling because the nightmare would only get better by talking it out.

14 Capture

As she, the Chief and Johnnie walked in Alex saw that Bill, Trey were with Trevor, and they were speaking to a woman that was probably the manager.

The Chief walked over and asked where the other guests might be and learned that a few were in the restaurant. He sent two of his men over with orders to keep the guests there.

Trevor shared the floor and room number and the Chief asked where the stairwells were located and sent two men to each location with instructions to keep people out of the stairwell or detain them if any came out.

He then suggested that he, Alex, and her team and two additional officers take the elevator up to the tenth floor.

On the way up, Alex learned from Trevor that Reston had rented the Grand Suite because it was the last available room. He had surprised the desk clerk by paying cash for the six hundred dollar per night rate and had paid for three days.

Alex let everyone in the elevator know that she wanted Reston alive and that she would take the lead in his arrest. Once he was subdued the Cleveland police should take over and make the official arrest.

The elevator door opened, and the gunfire started.

As she stepped out, she felt a bullet hit her in the right side. She shouted out to the people in the elevator not to shoot and then she shot Reston in the arm in which he was holding his gun. She followed with a shot to his left thigh. As he went down, she shouted for the team to subdue him.

Trey was the first to get to Reston and he kicked him in midsection as Reston tried to pick up his gun with his left hand.

The kick launched Reston against the wall. He was trying to breath and seemed to be mouthing curses.

Alex sat down against the wall. She knew she was going to have a huge bruise on her right side.

Bill knelt next to her and asked if she was alright. He said he knew exactly how she was feeling at the moment because he had felt that way on the previous day.

Alex gave him a weak smile and said that she was going to see if she could sit in the hot tub for the rest of the day, but she wanted to tell Reston that she was going to make sure he would get a fair trial and that she hoped he would be sent to the gas chamber or at least get life.

Bill helped her up and they walked around to where two deputies had hand cuffed Reston and read him his rights.

She looked at Reston and told him what an SOB he was. She surprised him by asking who at the front desk had let him know that they were on the way up. Alex suspected that someone at the front desk had informed Reston.

Reston smiled and said that she would need to determine on her own who the greedy person at the desk was.

He had given her confirmation about someone at the desk having called him. She looked at the Chief and asked him to detain all the office personnel.

She watched as the EMT personnel came out of the elevator. She walked over to them and said that she had been shot in the side, but the bullet had been stopped by her Kevlar jacket. She showed them the flattened bullet and asked if they carried Tylenol. She took two and thanked them when the lead EMT told her to keep the bottle.

She looked at the Chief and said that the rest of the action was all his, but she wanted to question the desk personnel before she left.

The Chief made several calls, and he then said that all the people in the hotel office were being detained.

Alex thanked him and signaled the team to the elevator.

When they got on the elevator, she thanked Trey for kicking Reston in the ribs for her.

Trey replied that if she had not let them know she wanted him alive, he would have kicked him harder.

Alex nodded and said that she knew how it felt to just want to kill someone and that she had put that urge to action when they had been kidnapped. Every person who aimed a gun at her had died.

Trevor smiled and said that was the time when he decided to only joke with her when they were in the office. He said he was afraid that on that day she would shoot anyone that made her mad.

Alex nodded and said that day was one of the lowest ones she had experienced in her life. She had watched Trey, who was on the verge of dying being helicoptered out by the EMT's.

Bill gave her a hug and said that he remembered that day and he still wondered how she had been able to subdue the entire group with only a broken piece of an armchair.

Alex smiled and said that she was sure that some frustrated angel was constantly trying to figure out how to keep her alive.

She led the way out of the elevator and went to the desk and addressed the five people that were behind it.

She showed them the hole in her jacket and the flattened bullet stuck to her Kevlar vest. She let them know that whoever had called up and given the person in the Royal Sweet warning that the police were on the way up should step forward voluntarily. She went on and let them know that not admitting it made them an accessory to attempted murder which carried a seven-to-fifteen-year prison sentence.

Admitting it would let them face a misdemeanor and they might face some community service as punishment.

There was a moment of silence and then one of the younger desk clerks said that he had made the call. He had just gotten the job and was short on cash. The two one-hundred-dollar bills had been too tempting to turn down. He had not expected the call to lead to her getting shot.

Alex asked if anyone else knew of the deal.

The other two clerks raised their hands.

Alex looked at the other two and asked the manager what she intended to do.

The manager said that she planned to fire all three.

Alex asked that she do her a favor and give them two weeks to go elsewhere.

She gave the three clerks her card that gave her Open Hands Foundation for young women address. She told the person who had taken the bribe that he should show up as well because she would have a job for him.

The manager shook her head and said that she admired her for being so generous to people that had caused her to be shot.

Alex replied that she lived her life with a simple guiding saying her mother had taught her, "Treat others the way you wish to be treated."

Alex then turned to the team and let them know that she wanted to question Reston once he got treated at the hospital and she again wanted to question the perp they had captured the day before.

She said she was going to sit in the hotel hot tub for most of the day and make it an early evening.

She let everyone know that they were free to go back to Cincinnati because the exciting action was over.

Trey let her know he was staying with her.

Trevor nodded and joked that he needed to get back to Cincy and spend some time with his kids.

Johnnie nodded and said the he needed to do the same.

Bill just shook his head and added, "ditto."

Alex led the way out to the curb and asked to be dropped off at the hotel.

When they got to the hotel, Trey said he would meet her by the hot tub and asked if there was anything he could do to make her feel better.

She smiled and replied that maybe the two of them should fall off their AA bandwagon and have a few shots of Jack Daniel.

Trey smiled and said that he knew the feeling, but they had worked too hard at staying sober to blow it.

Alex said that she agreed so maybe he could order in their favorite mix of Thai food to share for dinner.

Trey agreed to do it and then asked what more she hoped to learn from Reston and the other perp.

Alex replied that she wanted to know where Reston had been and what he had been doing. She added that she did not expect to get much from him but hoped that he had been lax about what he had in his hotel room.

She added that the person they had arrested the day before could most likely be flipped to provide some additional information but did not expect much other than general information about what had transpired at the processing site.

Trey arrived at the hot tub about an hour after returning to the hotel. He thought Alex was asleep in the hot tub.

Alex had called Matt and talked with him briefly and let him know what had happened. She then relaxed and closed her eyes.

She had her eyes closed but watched Trey enter. He was talking on his phone. She figured he was talking to Lindsey and maybe Nolan.

Trey said goodbye and sat on the edge of the hot tub and put his feet in.

Alex smiled and asked how everyone at home was.

Trey let her know that Lyndsey had wished her a quick recovery and Nolan had asked if she had shot the bad guy.

Alex shook her head and said she was getting a bad reputation with Nolan.

Trey smiled and let her know that she was Nolan's heroine and that he wanted to be just like her.

Alex replied that she would have to make sure he knew that she had graduated with a law degree. She figured he might like to become a judge.

Trey said he figured he would worry about that in a few years but for now he was just fine with who Nolan saw as a heroine.

15 Adjudication

For Alex, the next morning seemed to come immediately after she put her head on her pillow. She got up took a hot shower and then went down to breakfast where she met with Trey. She called and talked with the Cleveland Chief of police and asked what they had found in the hotel room.

The Chief said that he would send her pictures of the paperwork they had found and that they had also found a briefcase with one hundred and fifty-six thousand dollars of cash.

Alex asked the Chief to send the paperwork information to the Cincinnati Police computer. She thanked him for the information and asked where Reston happened to be. The Chief let her know that Reston would be brought to the Police station around noon and put in a holding cell.

Alex asked that he be kept away from the perp that they had arrested the day before.

She let him know that she would review the information that he had sent her and then be in to question the perp around nine.

She sent the information to Trey so the two of them could review what had been found. She sent the same information to Johnnie and asked him review it and see what more could be learned.

The fact that Reston had traveled to LA under the name of Preston Clemente and that a passport with that name had been found in his room indicated that Reston had been prepared with at least one fake ID. He had traveled first class, so his ego still needed to be fed.

She sent a note to Johnnie and ask him to see who had been seated next to Reston on the way out and on the way back from LA and let him know that she wanted to interview those persons. She also mentioned that the rental car information would most likely provide information about where in LA Reston had been.

Trey suggested that they should share the information with Reston so that he would know how detailed the investigation was going and that they would be questioning the people he had met with. He said that it might get him to inadvertently give them more information.

Trey's comments made Alex think about the fact that Johnnie could probably find the locations of the Mafia leaders in LA and with the rental car mileage information recreate the route that Reston might have driven.

Alex agreed and took a last sip of her coffee and said it was time to get to the station.

They caught a cab and were soon there. Alex was greeted by the same Seargent who greeted her by name but added, "the Candy Lady."

Alex nodded and after reclaiming her weapon led the way back to the Chief's office.

She declined the Chief's offer of coffee then shared her plans for the day. She let him know that she planned to either go back to Cincinnati or to fly to LA and contact the people that Reston had worked with. She Shared that she wanted to close down any operation that Reston might have been out there to help set up.

The Chief nodded and said he was impressed by the speed by which she worked and that if his office could be of any help it was at her disposal.

Alex thanked him and said she was ready to get going.

The Chief called in his support and asked her to show Alex to the holding cell area.

On the way Alex asked the support to check on the availability of flights to LA with a return to two or three days later back to Cincinnati and added that direct flights were preferred.

The officer in charge of the holding cell greeted her and validated her and Trey's identity and then led the way to an interview room.

He let her know that the perp would sit at the table across from the two of them but be chained to a holding ring and two officers would stay in the room with them.

Alex thanked him for the information and smiled as she asked whether the two officers were older and mean looking.

The officer in charge gave a small laugh and told her that the two were younger but he would ask them to scowl while in the questioning room.

Alex replied that she would have to work with that.

When Dario was led in and secured to the holding ring on the table he looked like he had not slept well.

Alex greeted him by name and let him know that he had two options. He could cooperate with her and willingly answer questions about the operation and get a much lighter jail sentence or he could plead the fifth but would most likely get the maximum sentence. She let him know that everything he said was being recorded and would be used in a court of law and asked him if he agreed to continue.

She asked him for his choice and his agreement.

Dario replied that he had not killed anyone.

Alex asked whether he had witnessed anyone being killed.

Dario was silent.

She looked up at the police officers and asked what the silence meant to them.

One of them replied that it made him believe that Dario had watched more than one killing.

Alex nodded and said that is what she thought as well. She looked at Trey and asked if he had any questions for Dario.

Trey nodded and asked who had done the killing.

Dario replied that Angelo had been the person who did most of the killing, but Luca had periodically come in and requested to be the one to do it.

Trey followed up by asking how many killings had occurred.

Dario was once again silent.

Trey looked at the police officers and asked how many killing might have taken place.

The other officer replied that he figured there must have been quite a few.

Alex asked Dario how he felt as he watched the killing.

Dario bowed his head and said that in made him sick and usually he closed his eyes. A few times he had to rush out of the room because he got sick. He said that Luca and Angelo teased him about his queasiness.

So, the killings bothered you. Why did you continued working there?

Dario shook his head and replied because he did not want to be one of the bodies delivered to the dissection table.

Alex nodded but said that he could have come to the police.

Dario nodded and replied that had he done so he would not have ended up on the table but would have been dead anyway.

Alex asked him if he believed there was a mole in the Cleveland police force.

Dario nodded and said that he was sure because he had heard Reston talking with that person. He did not know who it was but there was someone.

Alex said that she had experience with moles because she had found one in the Cincinnati police department that had almost ended her life. He was now dead and if she figured out who the mole was in the Cleveland police department he would at the least end up in prison.

She knew that the two police officers would spread the word, and she hoped the informant would be found out.

She then asked Dario why Reston had gone to LA.

Dario said that Reston had boasted about being asked to set up similar operations in LA, Asia, and Europe. He boasted that soon he would be promoted to be the leader of a global body parts organization.

Alex asked if Reston had gone to any place other than LA.

Dario shook his head and said that LA was the first place.

Alex asked if there was anything else that Dario wanted to share.

Dario nodded and said that Reston often sat in a viewing room watching the dissection and that once he had been present to watch the killing and preparation of a child.

Alex shook her head and asked how many children had they killed.

Dario replied that there was only one.

Alex asked how that had made him feel.

Dario shook his head and replied that it had made him sick, and he had rushed out of the room.

Alex leaned across the table and again asked why he had not gone to the police.

Dario nodded and said that he had thought about it, but the next day was when the shooting started, and he was arrested.

Alex sat down. She was shaking because she knew that if she had worked faster the child might still be alive.

Trey knew what was going through Alex's mind.

He announced that the questioning was over and that a formal arrest warrant needed to be filed and that Dario should be held without bail until trial.

Alex nodded and agreed. She looked at Dario and let him know that she would let the prosecutor know that he had voluntarily participated.

Dario thanked her as he was led out of the room.

Alex thanked Trey for taking over. She added that the questioning session had made the decision that they were going to LA.

She did not want the operation there to start up.

Trey said he agreed and that after they got done questioning Reston he was ready to go.

She led the way to the recording room and asked the technician there to send a copy to the Cincinnati police department.

When she and Trey entered his office, the police Chief asked whether they wanted to go out for a quick lunch or eat in the station cafeteria.

Alex replied that she trusted him to make the better choice.

He replied that he had a favorite Cuban restaurant where his favorite meal was a pig knuckle on a bed of yellow rice piled on top of black beans.

Alex smiled and asked Trey if he was ready for a pig knuckle.

Trey shook his head and said that he hoped that they had more on the menu than just pig knuckles.

The Chief laughed and said they had a great menu and even featured vegan meals.

He led the way out of his office and let his support know where they were going for lunch and that she should call him when Reston was brought over from the hospital.

On the way to the restaurant, Alex informed the Chief that he had a mole in his department.

The Chief asked her how she knew that.

Alex let him know that Reston had been overheard talking to that person.

The Chief replied that he would need to figure out how to find that person.

They arrive at the Cuban restaurant where the Chief was greeted at the door and led to his favorite table.

Alex liked the atmosphere of the place and felt like she had been there before.

The menu did not feature the pig knuckles, so Alex asked about it.

The Chief said that he had asked for that when he first came in and the chef had come out and asked him where he had learned about that dish.

The Chief had first experienced that dish when he was a student and the University of South Florida, in Tampa. He had shared that with the Chef who said that his grandfather had been the owner of the restaurant where he had first eaten pig knuckles.

Alex asked Trey if he was willing to share a plate with her.

Trey replied he had never eaten pig knuckle before but was willing to try.

The Chief ordered two pig knuckles, and they all agreed to an iced tea.

They chatted about life along Lake Erie and learned that the Chief had his own fishing boat and spent many a weekend out on the lake fishing.

Alex shared that she grew up along Lake Michigan and spent many a weekend with her father fishing. They owned a boat that he kept at a marina.

She showed him a picture of her prize catch.

He said he wished he had such a trophy but so far he had only caught regular sized fish.

The order for the table came.

Alex looked at the size of the serving and said she was glad she was sharing, and that Trey was a big eater.

She took the empty plate and scooped out the rice and beans and cut a piece of meat from the knuckle.

She ask Trey if he thought the two of them would be able to finish it.

Trey replied that he was going to see how the Chief handled it, but he was going to stop when he was full.

Alex said that she thought that what she had helped herself to was more than enough.

She checked to see if there were similar restaurants in Cincinnati and found several that had similar menus and that none had pig knuckles on the menu.

She was just commenting on that when the Chief got a call.

The Chief answered and exclaimed, "you have got to be kidding! Did they catch the shooter? How in the world would the mafia know that? I will be at the scene in fifteen."

He hung up and looked at Alex and said she was not going to believe what had just happened.

Alex replied that she figured that Reston had been killed.

The Chief looked at her and asked how she could have possibly guessed that.

Alex replied that she figured that the mafia did not want Reston to be alive. He had left Cincinnati because of the loss of the business there. He had just lost the Cleveland business and had been captured by the police.

The Chief nodded and said they he had to go to the scene but if they wanted to they could stay and casually finish lunch.

Alex replied that they would go with him.

On the way she asked who he had told about bringing Reston to the station.

The Chief was quiet for a few moments and then replied that he had only told the transport team and their boss about bring Reston to the station.

Alex replied that it could be one of them, but she wondered if his support knew about the transport.

He looked over at her and asked if she was suggesting that his support was the informant.

Alex said that she would ask her magician to check out his support's bank account and her spending habits.

She asked the Chief for his supports name and her home address.

He replied that he would give it to her when they arrived at the hospital.

When Alex had the information she called Johnnie and informed him about what had happened and asked him to dig into the supports finances and spending habits.

Johnnie replied that, "he would have what she was asking for in a few."

Alex walked over to where Reston was slumped in the wheelchair, being examined by the coroner, and getting his picture taken by the coroners team.

She looked at the scene and commented that the mafia had just saved the state a lot of money by killing the person that she figured would potentially spend life in prison.

The coroner looked at her and commented that she was being a little cold hearted.

Alex replied that when he found out what the person in the wheelchair had done he would agree with her sentiment.

The Chief walked the scene and then came over to where Alex and Trey were and suggested they go back to his office. He wanted to follow up on Alex's identification of the potential mole.

Alex suggested they stop for an ice cream so that her magician had time to discover the information that would give the Chief the winning hand.

<u>*16 West Coast*</u>

The Chief was silent as he drove to Melanies Ice Cream Shop. He led the way in and commented that he was going down the list of ice cream flavors. He said he was about a third of the way down the list. He added that so far he like every flavor.

Alex replied she was going with one scoop of raspberry and one scoop of strawberry.

Trey ordered a dark chocolate and a scoop of coffee ice cream.

They found a table and sat down.

The Chief commented that the coroner had shared Alex's comment, and he had let the coroner know that he agreed with her and that the comment was an appropriate one. The coroner said he needed to find out what the person he was taking to the morgue had done.

Alex took another spoon of her ice cream then added that the incident had helped her decide that she and Trey were going to go to LA to see if they could prevent a body parts business from opening up there. She asked if she and Trey could use the facilities at the station to freshen up prior to going to the airport.

The Chief replied that would be an easy request to fill. He then volunteered to personally drive them to the Airport.

Alex thanked him and as she was finishing the last spoon of ice cream her phone buzzed.

She smiled as she listened to Johnnie as he commented that her last request had been easy to fulfill.

She asked him to hold for a moment and that she was going to walk out of the ice cream shop with the Chief to his car where she would put him on speaker phone.

She led the way out to the car and then asked Johnnie to share his findings.

Johnnie said that the support had not tried to hide her new financial gain, or she was not aware that her spending was out stripping her earnings. She was consistently withdrawing cash from her US bank, and her account always had a new deposit from a bank in Jamaica. Johnnie was able to confirm that the Jamaican bank was getting a thirty thousand a month deposit. It was as if she had a straight hose to a cash machine and she was spending freely. He wondered what she was buying.

The Chief spoke up and said he believed it might be clothes, shoes and purses and other personal items. He had recently complemented her on one of her black pants suits.

Alex asked Johnnie to hold for a moment so she could give him the correct connection to the Cleveland computer center where he could send what he had found. She asked the Chief to have his IT send the connection information to Johnnie. Once that was settled she thanked Johnnie for having worked one of his miracles and let him know she was headed for LA.

Johnnie asked whether he could share what he had found with the rest of the team.

Alex replied that was a good next step.

The Chief shook his head and said that he could not believe his office was the direct source of the leak. He wondered how long that arrangement had gone on.

Alex said that he would be able to get that information from what Johnnie sent him. Alex added he would need to have his support volunteer most of the information to be used in court. She let him know Johnnie was her magician not her court information provider.

The Chief smiled and said that he understood and that he would keep the information he got from Johnnie to the side and use it as a guide to get what he needed to nail his support.

Alex said she understood his anger and that he would benefit from a call from her Chief.

She followed the Chief into the building as he seemed to be rushing to his office. Along the way he asked two officers to accompany him.

The Chief stopped in front of the receptionist and asked her to stand up. He then addressed her by name, "Connie Francis Mandolin, you are under arrest."

He pointed to one of the officers and asked him to read her the Miranda rights. He asked the other to handcuff her and take her to a holding cell.

He told her that he was going to charge her for leaking sensitive information to the mafia and she should be thinking about how to save her own hide.

Connie began by saying she was sorry.

The Chief put up his hand and told the two to take her away.

Alex nodded, and said, "sorry to be caught but not yet truly sorry for my sins."

She and Trey followed the Chief into his office.

The Chief looked at some papers on his desk and hand them to Alex. It was the plane reservations to LA. He commented that his folks did not get to ride first class.

Alex smiled and said that she personally paid for the first-class upgrade cost differential because she had a phobia about getting caught somewhere in the middle or back of the plane.

She said that he would understand if he came to Chicago, met her family, and went out with her fishing that she had personal wealth to be able to do so. She did not say anything about the fact that much of the money she had come from a personal friend that was the wife of the leader of a Mexican drug cartel that she had killed.

She looked at the tickets reservation information and said that this information was most likely in the hands of the Mafia. She asked if there was another support who could make similar reservations on another airline that might arrive to LA close to the same time.

The Chief nodded, made a call and a few moments later a Black male support entered the room.

He looked at her and smiled as he listened to the Chief's instruction.

He said he understood the request and he was honored to be making reservations for, "Cincinnati's Black Annie Oakley." "I am Samual Jefferson, and I have recorded every news article that has been presented about your various cases, and I am going to find you the best seats available he went on," as he gave her a little bow.

Alex thanked him and asked him to do the best he could in getting her out of Cleveland and to call her Alex.

The Chief looked at her and said he wondered about the attitude of his police force and said that the word must be out about her. He was sure her action at the hotel had made the rounds. He had caught many of them stopping to look at us as we went past them.

Trey smiled and replied that it was really hard to be a backup for a super heroine and though he had much longer legs he found it hard to keep up with her.

Alex shook her head and said that the Chief should not listen to Trey and that he was a decorated Marine who had been awarded a purple heart and had a metal of honor for his service in Iraq.

The Chief said that both of them were heroes in his eyes.

Alex asked about the locker room and was soon standing under a hot shower, letting the days tension drain away as she thought about how to handle what she might find in LA. Her bruise from the bullet hit made its presence known.

She got dressed in fresh comfortable clothes in which to travel. She always included a suit jacket so she could conceal her weapon. She was first to the cafeteria and bought a bottle of water and sat down. A few moments later Trey walked in. He was wearing the same jacket he had which let her know that he had not brought any extra ones.

She waited until he sat down and let him know that if he needed any clothing they could stop at some shop at the airport, and she would buy them and later expense them.

Trey thanked her but said that he had everything he needed.

Alex pointed out the support approaching them.

Samuel sat down next to her and said that he had found a flight earlier then the pervious reservation. It had a connection in Atlanta and then a non-stop to LA. It only got in an hour before the one from Cleveland. He said he was shocked by the price and had called up the airlines special services and let them know that it was two police agents making the flight but was only able to get a couple of hundred dollars trimmed off.

Alex thanked him for the help, put her ticket into her vest pocket, and handed the other ticket to Trey.

She thanked Samuel for getting the reservation changed so quickly and for his effort at getting the price reduced.

She led the way out of the cafeteria and found her way to the Chief's office. She said that she and Trey were ready to go to the airport. She asked for a plain white envelope.

On the way out of the building, she asked the Chief if there was a money machine available. She stopped and took out several hundred dollars. She put a one-hundred-dollar bill into the envelope, put Samuels full name on the front, and put a message on the flap, "Your share of the trimmings."

She handed it to the building receptionist and asked that the envelope be given to the Samuel.

The Chief asked if she were bribing his office help.

Alex smiled and said it all balanced out. She was helping send one office help to hell and the other momentarily to heaven.

The Chief thanked her and led the way to his car. He let her know that he had talked to her Chief and had brought him up to date. He got the impression that she got to do pretty much what she decided to do.

She replied that she always made sure to make her Chief be the face of her cases. He had become one of the most supported detective unit Chiefs and was on the way to getting promoted. She added that she followed her mother's advice of always making the boss happy.

The Chief smiled and said that he was very interested in meeting her mother so he could personally get some advice from a very smart woman.

Alex smiled and said that he should send her the recipe for the Cuban dish he liked so much because her mother was also a renowned Chef.

"Wow, a wise woman and a Chef, your father is a lucky man," the Chief commented as he pulled the car into the drop off area.

He got out and shook both Trey and her hand.

Alex reached up and gave him a hug. She thanked him for making the stay in Cleveland enjoyable.

She then turned and pulled her bag and headed to the check-in area.

Once they checked in Alex led the way to the Airline lounge. Once they were inside and seated with a snack and a drink she said they should exit their plane in LA in their full Kevlar body suit. She did not expect anything to happen in the airport, but she wanted them to each buy a hat with a large brim and to put on their Kevlar head gear when they exited to get to their cab. She added that she would see if she could arrange to be picked up away from where everyone gathered to catch a cab. She was afraid if they were in the crowd the people around them were at risk.

Trey said if she had a premonition of trouble he was all in on being prepared. He commented that the Kevlar outfit was a bit warm and hoped the airplane would be kept on the cool side.

Alex said that she was carrying on her Kevlar top, head gear and socks but would wear the pants. She would put on the rest once they were in the airport in LA.

The wait in Atlanta was short and the Flight to LA was long but comfortable. They both caught some sleep and were ready when they landed. After a stop in the restroom to put on the rest of the Kevlar protection, they were ready to head for the exit.

Alex stopped at a shop that featured hats in its display window. She led the way in and after a brief search she picked the hat with the biggest brim. It completed covered her face. She then helped Trey select his hat. It was a straw hat that had a huge droopy brim. She laughed and said if he sat down people would think he was taking a siesta.

Trey asked her to take a picture so he could send it home.

Alex called for an Uber and asked to be picked up out front where the luggage was delivered to the passengers.

She stopped and pulled on her head gear and put on her hat. She looked at Trey and said he looked like he was starring in the invisible man movie.

Trey responded that she had completely disappeared.

Alex waited until the large SUV with an Uber designation got to the curb before exiting to the curb. It seemed to her that almost immediately Trey pushed her forward, and she hit the side of the SUV. He then pulled her to the ground and pushed her to the back wheel. They each got behind a wheel as several bullets penetrated the SUV roof and hit the sidewalk behind them.

Trey shouted out that a sniper was on some rooftop where he had clear site of them and told Alex to stay down.

Just as Alex thought it was over a van came racing by and a shooter laying on top sprayed the SUV with machine gun fire. Alex kept her head down as she felt the bullets impacts hitting the SUV

Alex heard a host of police sirens and as she stood up carefully to look around a policeman behind her shouted for her to turn around with her hands in the air.

She did as instructed but suddenly the officer was hit. She took off her hat and headgear and quickly ran to him to stop the bleeding that was near his neck.

The officer looked up at her and asked whether she was the good guy.

She nodded in the affirmative.

Trey had taken off his head gear and was holing up his badge shouting for everyone to stay back.

Alex told the officer that she was on his side.

She put compression on the wound and got the bleeding to stop. She asked the officer how he was feeling and that she could see the EMT van approaching, and they would soon have him on the way to the hospital.

As the EMT team took over, she and Trey were both asked for their ID's.

Alex let the officer in charge know that she and Trey were armed but had not used their weapons.

They were both asked for their weapons.

After a brief discussion Alex suggested that they all go to the nearest police station where they would be safe from any additional shooting.

The officer in charge of the scene made a call and then instructed them to get into one of the police cars.

The driver of the SUV rushed up and asked about the damage to his SUV.

Alex said that she would make sure he was compensated but that for the near future it would be states evidence. She added that she would make sure he had another SUV so that he could make a living.

The driver said that there were so many bullet holes in the van that he was not sure he would ever be able to use it again.

The officer let her know that the SUV would later be taken to the station. He said that the driver would be questioned to see what he knew or had observed.

Alex and Trey got into the police car. She commented that she was glad they had slept on the way because the rest of the day was going be hectic.

At the station she was taken to an office with a sign identifying it as the Commandant of the LA airport police.

Alex and Trey were seated in front of the Commandant's desk, and they were asked for their identification.

Alex introduced Trey and then herself and said they were on the way to disrupt a hideous business the Mafia was setting up in LA and that speed was critical. She pointed out that the shooting highlighted how the Mafia felt about the two of them arriving in LA.

The Commandant asked what type of business she was trying to stop.

Alex handed him a phone number and asked him to call her boss, the Chief of Detectives in Cincinnati, and let him determine what she was allowed to share.

The commandant made the call. After some introductions and sharing the situation in LA he asked what type of assignment the two detectives he had sitting in the office were on. He shook his head and said that he was not aware of such a business and that it was a horrible one to contemplate.

He said he understood and would make sure they had all the support they needed.

After hanging up he said he was going to make a couple of calls so that they would have some backup if they needed it.

Alex nodded. Her phone buzzed. She knew that it was the Chief. She excused herself and went just outside of the office.

The Chief asked how she was feeling and then added that he wanted to make sure that she was getting the support he asked for.

Alex let him know that the attitude had changed from one of challenge to support.

The Chief told her to be extra careful because the mafia must see her as a potent threat that needed to be eliminated.

Alex thanked him for his help and let him know that she was making sure he was being kept in the loop.

She re-entered the room and sat back down in her chair.

The Commandant said that her Boss made the request that the LA police provide all the support that they could afford, and that Alex was trying to stop the Mafia from setting up a human body parts processing and distribution center. He said that seemed like a horrible business.

He shook his head and said that he would make sure she had the support she needed and that two units were on the way and would be at her disposal. She could determine how close to keep them but suggested that they always were only a couple of blocks away.

He let her know that the two units would be out at the curb in a few moments.

He asked what they planned to be driving.

Alex let him know that she had rented one of the larger model cars but did not know what she would drive out of the lot. She would make sure her two units knew what she was driving and the license plate number.

She thanked the Commandant and asked if they could get a ride to the rental car lot with one of their support units.

The Chief nodded and said that would be no problem and walked with them out to the curb.

He asked the four officers to get out of their cars and made introductions. He instructed them to give close support to Alex and Trey but to stay about two blocks away.

One of the officers said that he had learned of Alex's reputation for action from a friend he had on the Cincinnati police department and was pleased to have been asked to back her up.

Alex let them know that the morning's event was enough for her, but she would do what was necessary and appreciated their help.

The Chief held the back door of one of the units and wished her good luck.

A few moments later they arrived to the car rental facility. Alex asked the two units to stay put and she would drive around and let them get a good look at the car she rented. She followed the signs and took the elevator to the floor where the car rental was located. She asked Trey which car he preferred.

He picked a converted Chevy Suburban.

Alex nodded and said she liked being in a big car.

After getting their car out of the parking lot Trey drove around to where the two police cruisers were parked.

He got out and went over to where the four officers were standing.

Alex said she would make a call to Johnnie to find out if he had found out where Reston had gone while he was in LA.

Johnnie gave her the route that he had figured out from the mileage on the car and studying the map and the buildings in several warehouse areas. He commented that Reston had gone to several warehouse locations. He figured that Reston had been looking at the different locations so he could pick the most suitable one.

He gave Alex the address of the three and suggested the address that seemed most likely. Two of the locations were new warehouse construction that Johnnie termed prefabricated warehouses, but the third address was one of an old brick and mortar warehouse, it was on the small side as compared to the much larger ones and it was on sale at a reduced price.

Alex thanked Johnnie and let him know she was going to drive by the first two and planned to stop at the third.

17 Los Angelos

Alex walked over to where Trey was chatting with the four policemen. She said that she had three warehouse addresses that she wanted to go to. She let them know that the first two addresses would be drive by and the last would be an actual stop. She shared that all three warehouses were either listed to sell or to lease and that the last address was for the oldest and smallest warehouse and the only one to be built out of brick.

She and Trey would see if they could gain entrance to it so they could inspect the interior.

She said that they should stay within sight of the SUV until they approached the third warehouse. Then they should drop back and stay out sight.

Trey led the way to the SUV. Once they were underway he asked how sure she was about the third warehouse.

Alex said that they should wear their full body armor.

Trey nodded and said that he would be ready for action.

The drive-by of the first two warehouses visually confirmed what Johnnie had shared with her.

As they approached the third warehouse Alex noted that there were several cars in the parking lot. One them was a black stretch a limousine.

Alex called back to the police squads following and said that they were driving by but would turn around and park in the street and approach the warehouse on foot. She suggested that the two squad cars park immediately behind the SUV and the four get out and get ready for action because there were cars in the parking lot and one of them was a limousine. She stated that it most likely meant that the mob boss was in the building.

She asked them to put on their body armor.

She planned to surprise the folks inside and added that she doubted they would be welcomed. She said she would leave her phone on so they could hear what was going on and if any shooting started they should enter immediately.

Trey led the way. He pointed to the black limo and said that the driver was most likely sitting in the car waiting.

Alex approached from one side and Trey the other. She knocked on the driver's window and when he rolled it down she put a gun in his face and instructed him to get out.

She called for the officers to come and arrest the driver.

Once he was being taken back to the police cruiser, Alex continued the approach to the warehouse.

Trey was in front as they approached a door, and he slowly opened the it.

He waved and then stepped in and to the side.

She did the same and stepped to the other side.

They were in a large empty part of the warehouse that had two truck doors at the back right side. There was a regular door and a truck door at the other end of the room. The brick wall seemed to be new.

Alex signaled for Trey to go around the truck entrance side, and she would go around the other side toward the regular door that was on her side.

She got to the door and waited for Trey to get to where she was standing.

She slowly opened the door and stepped in with Trey immediately at her heals.

The scene in front of them stopped them cold.

Alex counted seven people in the room. Two were pulling a young Black woman who was struggling, toward a stainless-steel table. There was one person at the table with a knife and there were two men who were apparently bodyguards to the third person who fit the stereotype of a mob boss. There was a person standing with the mob boss with his hands crossed at his back that seemed to be a spectator.

Alex shouted out that they were all under arrest and to put up their hands.

For a moment everything seemed to freeze in place.

Then the two bodyguards turned to shoot.

Alex knew that she had only one shot per person, so she shot the two gunmen in the forehead then she dropped to the floor as the rest of the group except the spectator pulled out a weapon and began to fire.

Alex took out the two closest to the young woman.

Trey took out the person who had been holding the knife.

Alex shouted out for Trey not to kill the leader, and she shot him in the gun arm and once in his thigh.

The two of them rushed forward.

Alex gave the young woman a hug and let her know she was safe.

Trey had hand cuffed the leader.

The four officers came rushing in looked around and made a call for an ambulance and for the coroner. One of the other officers called in for a search warrant to be brought out to the site. The other asked the young woman about what had happened. He recorded the fact that she had gone shopping for groceries and was loading her car when she was pulled into a van and had a hood pulled over her head. When the hood was removed she was in the cell. She had spent the night sitting in the cell and this morning the guy who had been standing at the table had let her know that she was to be the first person that would inaugurate the new West Coast human body parts business.

She broke down and said that she had refused to come out of the cell and had fought the two guys pulling her toward the table.

The mafia boss sat on the floor holding one hand on the bullet hole in his thigh and the other over the bullet hole through his arm. He cursed her and asked how she had found out where the operation was being set up.

Alex waited to reply while one of the officers arrested him and read him his rights.

Alex shook her head and said that she had a magician working for her, but what he should be worried about was which prison or gas chamber he would be visiting. She told him that her magician would find out about all the wrongdoing he had been involved in, and he would either spend the rest of his life in prison, visit the gas chamber or have one of his bosses send word to eliminate him when they found he had been flipped and was for the law.

Alex and Trey each put their guns into evidence bags and then gave each other a hug.

Alex complemented Trey, who in turn complemented her and said he was glad she left a couple of shots for him.

The mafia boss sneered at her and said neither she nor anyone else would get him to flip.

Alex smiled and replied that she wasn't going to try to get him to flip she would just make sure the media got the message that he had.

He cursed her as he was being put into the ambulance.

Alex walked over to where the young lady was being questioned by one of the officers. She checked to make sure that she was alright and had someone who would be meeting her. She then introduced herself and then gave her one of her Helping Hands cards and told her it was a foundation that helped young women through tough times and that she was welcome to stay for a few months at no charge. She should call the number on the card to make all arrangements, and it would all be a free service.

The woman introduced herself as Daniela Brickly and replied that at the moment getting out of LA was the one thing she wanted to do.

Alex gave her a hug and told her she would be welcome in Ohio.

She walked over to the officer that seemed to be in charge and asked him if she and Trey could leave.

He replied that his instructions were to secure the site and when the search warrant was granted to search the entire facility and secure the warehouse. He had been informed that she and her partner could do whatever they wanted except search the site.

Alex nodded and said she had no desire to go anywhere in the warehouse, but she was going to see about getting a flight home.

She led the way out to the SUV where she leaned against it and asked Trey if he was ready to go back to the waterpark and finish the picnic that they had been called away from.

Trey nodded and asked if that picnic had occurred in this current year. He added that he felt that he had been aged a few years by the horror of the case.

Alex replied that only two months and ten years had elapsed, and they were both a lot older.

The End

Preview of: The Skull Collector

1 Skull Collector

*L*evi lay on the lawn enjoying the concert and playing visual games with the clouds passing overhead. Once in a while one would trigger a memory. He was slowly thinking through and visualizing the first time.

He remembered his fascination with Heather. He was always standing just down from her locker so he could get a look at her when she was getting ready for the next class. It was during the late summer football practice when the cheerleaders came out for their practice that he finally went over the edge. Heather was thrown in the air and then landed on the shoulders of the guy that had thrown her up. Her hair had flown back, and her perfect features had been exposed. Her smile that he was sure was meant for him had closed the deal.

It was the moment that his mind seemed to clear, and he knew what he wanted. He wanted Heather to be with him forever.

He spent the next few weeks figuring out how that could happen.

He found a place in the forest that was at one end of the farm. He prepared the grave. He made sure it was dug neatly and to the proper depth. He wanted it to be a perfect place.

He then waited patiently. The school session started, and he kept watch as he waited for the right time. Then one day Heather came to her locker alone to put her books away. She had just locket it and was going toward the gym with her gym bag.

He walked up and said hello. She stopped, smiled, and asked what he wanted. He replied that he wanted to take her out on a date. Her smile caused his heart to beat twice as fast.

He knew she was going to turn him down, so he took the next step. He pulled out his hunting knife and pressed it against her side and told her to walk out the door and guided her to where he had his old pickup parked.

She said he was hurting her.

He told her to be quiet and walk. He put his arm over her shoulder, and they walked slowly to the pickup. He told her to get in, and he slammed the door shut. She tried to open it, but he had removed the inside handles for both the door and the window. He hurried to his side and got in, started the engine, and drove slowly away and headed toward the farm.

Heather reached for the steering wheel trying to make him go off the road.

He pulled the chloroform-soaked cloth from the plastic bag and clamped it over her mouth.

Heather went out as she tried to pull his hand away.

He drove down the lane toward the house and then took the small gravel road that led to the lake and pulled in next to the grave. He looked to make sure his dad was not fishing. He heard the tractor and knew that his dad was most likely out pulling the John Deer multiple row hoe that cleared five corn rows at a time. He knew that he had all the time in the world, and he should enjoy what he planned to do next.

He pulled on his hip high fishing waders to make sure he didn't get any blood on his clothes. He then lay Heather face down and with his hunting knife he cut her throat. He was amazed at the amount of blood that kept pumping out. Every year his dad butchered at least one large pig, and he always hung the pig up and then cut its throat to bleed it. He had not expected so much blood from such a petite body as Heather's.

Once the pulse bleeding stopped, he reached down and cut off her head and rolled the body into the grave. He threw her gym bag down after her. He kneeled down and skinned her head and threw all the fleshy parts down into the grave. He rolled the skull around so he could get a good view from the front. He threw it into the plastic five-gallon bucket that was half full of diluted lye water. He put on the lid and made sure it was against the back corner by the tailgate.

He walked to the lake to wash the blood that was on his waders until he was sure that it was all off. He then took them off and put on his sneakers.

He then filled in the grave and put a layer of leaves and several limbs over it to camouflage it. He stood back and admired his work. It looked like the rest of the forest floor. He figured that by spring it would be unnoticeable.

He drove back to the small barn and looked around to make sure no one was looking and carried the bucket in and took it up to the loft and put it behind some old hardware that had been untouched for years. He would come back in a few days to see how Heather's skull looked.

He went into the house where his mother asked him how school had been. He replied that it had been a great day and sat down for his afternoon snack that she always had ready.

He realized he had been daydreaming when the concert music he was listening to ended and the crowd gave a thunderous applause.

He sat back up and once again looked at the two women he had scoped out.

He gave up on his first selection when it was clear that she had someone with her.

He kept his focus on his second choice. He followed her out of the park and watched the direction she was walking in.

Lisa was walking home after the free concert in the field and didn't realize the mistake she had made until it was too late. It was a long walk home and it was getting dark when she accepted a ride. The driver of the black pickup seemed friendly and as she got in; he asked her where she needed to go.

She put on the seat belt as he requested and gave him her address. She was about to thank him when he sprayed something at her. It was the last thing she saw as the world slowly went dark.

Levi smiled and opened the window on the passenger's side to let the fresh air in. He had perfected using the spray bottle to deliver the chloroform. It sometimes made him woozy, but he had learned to hold his breath while he was spraying his prize with it.

He reached over and pulled the young woman's hair back so he could get a good look at her profile. He liked what he saw and imagined what her skull would look like once he processed and mounted it.

He headed straight to the processing center where he would sell her body for a cool fifty thousand dollars. He would keep the head. This was a deal he had set up with the Body Parts manager that would have her chopped up and sell her body parts. He was sure the he was only getting about ten percent of what her body was worth but for years he had to do the hard work of burying the bodies. Now he was getting paid a nice sum and he walked away with a clean skull.

He had called and let them know he was at the door. The warehouse door opened, and he drove in.

He followed as they took her to the next room, put her on the table and undressed her and cut off her hair and bagged it. They said that he was in luck and the doctor that did the dissecting was expecting her in the next room.

He would take the scalp, the ears, eyes and tongue and facial skin and they would bring back the head for him. They said the boss would bring out the money.

This was his third delivery. He was now doing about one delivery every other week. He knew that it was risky to be harvesting so many skulls, but he was strategic about it and made sure he picked up his targets in different county jurisdictions and from quite different venues.

He had picked up one guy by mistake but decided to collect him anyway. Most of his skulls were of women but he had accumulated three of young men. He actually thought the three male skulls were appealing because they were noticeably larger than the rest of his trophies.

Delivery to this local facility was very convenient, and the money was more icing on the cake then he had ever dreamt of.

He had made what he had at first thought was accidental contact at a nearby bar with the person running the operation. He learned later that he had actually been targeted to be a victim to become some of the body parts but somehow during the conversation he had connected with the person who ran the operation he had asked if the body parts business needed any bodies. He had been invited to bring in a body.

He had been surprised by the change in the conversation but the person making the invitation promised that it was a legitimate offer, and the money was substantial.

He had taken his next prize in and had gotten a tour of the operation and an offer of fifty thousand per body. The arrangement was not only financially attractive, but it was even more alluring because he did not have to go through the effort of digging a grave and preparing the skull. It saved him time and a tremendous amount of work.

His father had died a couple of years before, and his mother had passed away the previous year. He missed them both. They had been good parents. He had fond memories of the many family outings and vacations that they had taken him on during his early teen years. But their passing made it much easier to pursue his main interest of collecting skulls.

He moved from the family farm to an old mansion that he had renovated with the money he got from his parents. He thought it was remarkable that they had saved three million dollars to pass on to him. He smiled as he thought about the fact that they were not only good parents but amazingly frugal.

He hired a professional farming group to run his farm, and he had the farmhouse refurbished and then had a rental agency manage it. This provided him with a steady cash stream that allowed him to invest all of his inheritance with a local investment firm.

He figured he would not have to work for the rest of his life and could focus on his fishing trips to Lake Cumberland, hunting in the fall and going to concerts, plays and sports events as he hunted out his next victim.

He felt that he had been rewarded for being good in his early youth.

Hunting for the next victim was the sport that he liked the best because it was done in different venues and the selection varied significantly. He always kept his eye out for that exceptional looker that had great hair and was gullible enough to accept a ride from him.

He knew that his good looks and a reassuring smile were key in getting them to accept a ride.

He was now at the Cincinnati River front attending a concert in the park. He was hoping to get his next prize that evening.

He had an eye on a young Black woman sitting out on the lawn and a young blond sitting almost to the top back of the inclined lawn. They both had the look that he wanted. He liked the Black woman the best and figured he would make a move on her when the concert ended.

Alex was sitting next to Matt and enjoying the concert that had been sponsored by one of the large Cincinnati companies. She let him know that she felt that someone was watching her.

Matt asked her if she wanted another iced tea and that he would see if he could spot anyone that seemed to be watching her.

She thanked him and said she would love a refill.

Matt got up and walked slowly to where the portable refreshment stand was parked.

Levi took note of the tall rather handsome Black man standing up and walking toward him. He remained seated but made sure not to look at him or the young woman who he had been sitting with. He wondered if he had been made.

Matt walked by and went over to the refreshment stand and purchased two iced teas and two chocolate ice cream cones. He casually scanned the crowd on the way back.

When he sat down, he let Alex know that he had spotted three potential guys that were alone and looking over the crowd.

Alex thanked him, took a sip of the iced tea, and said that the ice cream cone was just what she needed.

Levi decided that the blond sitting by herself would be the one he would try to intercept. He would invite her to a treat and if she accepted would then invite her to one of the local clubs for a drink.

He made sure not to look at the Black lady again.

It was his lucky night. The young woman took him up on his offer of an ice cream cone and afterwards a drink. She said that she had a club in mind.

He knew he had scored when she selected the place to get a drink. He needed to play it low key and to be as invisible as possible at the club.

Alex had a feeling that something was wrong. She walked out scanning the crowd trying to see if anyone seemed distressed. She saw several young people mingling and talking. Everything seemed to be OK.

Levi seemed to sense that he was being looked at and made sure to keep his back to the departing crowd. He focused on getting the young lady to accept him as someone she wanted to have a few drinks with.

Alex asked Matt if he would later be able to identify the three guys that he had observed.

Matt replied that he thought so. One had red hair and lots of freckles. One had blond hair and was rather young looking and the other had dark brown eyes and he thought brown hair, but that person had his sweatshirt hood on, so it was hard to tell hair color.

Alex nodded and took his hand, and they walked back to their apartment.

Levi and the lady that had identified herself as Elsy walked to a local night spot that had a small dance floor where they drank and danced until close to closing time. Levi did not want to be the last to leave the bar, so he offered to drive her home.

She accepted saying that it would save her a walk up to Mount Adams.

Levi was thrilled. Once in the truck he sprayed Elsy with his chloroform spray. She went out like a light.

It was three in the morning. He had been drinking iced tea in a whiskey glass, so he was ready for the drive up to Cleveland. He would get there early in the morning and be home to have a late lunch. He had been disappointed when the Body Parts operation moved to Cleveland, but the drive was a minor inconvenience relative to doing everything himself to collect the skull.

He figured when he got back to Cincinnati, he would do Chinese carryout for a late afternoon meal and then spend the rest of the evening preparing her skull.

He drove a little over the speed limit but made sure there were other cars driving faster.

The timing of the delivery went off as planned.

He parked in the alley on the side of the house opposite the main street. Two new guys came out and took her in.

He had a short wait, but he soon left the operation with the money and his head that he put in the large toolbox in the back of the truck.

He was just getting back to Cincinnati when a cop turned on the red lights and pulled him over.

He briefly entertained making a run for it and if he had been out by his farm he would have because he figured he knew how to out fox any cop on the roads there. But he pulled over and kept his hands on the steering wheel.

One cop shouted for him to get out and stand behind the pickup. The other walked up to the passenger window and looked in. He then went around to the driver's side and examined the inside more closely.

Levi hoped that he would not get inspected too closely.

He presented his driver's license and listened to the officer that said he had been doing sixty-five in fifty-five-mile zone. He was asked if he had any alcohol in the pickup.

Levi was glad that he had not stopped to stock up on beer. He only had an iced tea from the big Mac in the pickup.

The officer looking inside of the pickup said it was clear.

He was asked to close his eyes and touch his nose with both index fingers.

He did that with no problem.

The officer nodded and said OK and wrote out the speeding ticket and advised him that he should stick to the speed limit.

The two cops got back into their unit and waited for him to go on his way.

He was so glad that he had no outstanding tickets. He had only one ticket in his life that he had gotten when he was sixteen.

Levi got back into his pickup and drove away doing fifty-five and being passed by every car on the highway. He figured that the cops were getting in their quota of speeding tickets. He knew that the ticket would cost him somewhere around three-hundred dollars, but he was so relieved that no detailed search had been done that he smiled and thanked the lord for small favors.

He then focused his thoughts on the upcoming processing of the head. This was the part he especially enjoyed. He was pleased that the body processing group always wanted the eyes, the tongue, the ears, and the scalp. That made his cleaning of the skull easy, and he did not have to deal with a bunch of waste to dispose of. The disposal had been reduced to scraping the flesh off the skull, boiling that residue, and then putting it down the sink through the garbage disposal.

The rest of the processing involved bleaching the skull and the mounting it. He enjoyed making the small plaque that had the young lady's picture a brief description of his time with her and the date of her beheading.

When he moved into his current home, he had converted the entire third floor into his display floor. It had a beautiful wood floor that had star patterns positioned strategically around the rooms. He had display pedestals made that were then positioned on each star. He had organized all the skulls in order of the date and had put each skull on its own separate pedestal. He was proud of the way he had arranged the layout and the spot lighting for each pedestal.

He wished he could give tours of his collection. He thought of the collection as a show of high art.

Many of his evening hours were spent walking the third floor and recalling the events leading to him getting each of his trophies.

The first floor had an entry area that he had arranged using the same pedestals as on the third floor but instead of heads he had put fake statues of Greek and Roman nude women.

The morning after the conference at breakfast, Alex shared the fact that she had a nightmare about the feeling of being watched the day before. She shared that she had one of her premonitions about the situation and was going to be extra careful for a few days until she could sort out what was going on.

Matt said he would be sure to keep a watch to make sure none of the three guys were around.

She took her bike down as usual and met Johnnie at the elevator. She asked him to pick a route to work that they usually did not take.

Johnnie asked what was going on.

Alex briefly shared what had happened.

Johnnie nodded and said he would pick a different route.

Once in the office, as they all sat down for their morning coffee and rolls Johnnie asked Alex to go into more detail about the concert in the park.

Alex described the situation and said that she had a dream about it and woke up in the morning with a premonition of trouble.

Trevor shook his head and said he hated it when she got her premonitions because so far, every time, she had one the team was faced with a major gun battle.

Trey said that he agreed but that every time they had all been prepared for the resulting gun battle and they, working together, had weathered every one of them.

He added that in every one of those situations Alex had taken the point and led them to victory. He also highlighted the number of times when she had been attacked while by herself and she had taken out her attacker.

Alex shook her head and said that this premonition was different, and the difference was what was bothering her.

The Chief came out of his office and joined them. He shared that he had just gotten off the phone with their friend, the Chief of Police of Loveland, who wanted to see if Alex and Trey would be able to stop by around lunch time. He wanted the two to meet a friend that was dealing with three missing young women each who had gone riding or hiking alone in different parts of the county and had never returned home.

Alex shook her head as she wondered if the lunch meeting would lead to what was bothering her. She said that she and Trey would go to Loveland for lunch.

She looked at Johnnie and asked if he was willing to come along to hear the story because she had a bad feeling about the meeting. She said that she wanted him to look for any missing women who had not returned from the concert in the park.

2 A Nagging Feeling

*A*lex sat in the passenger seat of her car as Trey drove to Loveland. She went through each of the previous cases where she and the team had intervened in situations where young women were about to get abused before being killed. It haunted her that during the time it took to break each of those cases young women had faced the situation by themselves, had been brutalized and then killed. This fact always came up when she engaged in a new case and the desire to solve the case as rapidly as possible became a key consideration. She had that feeling now. She was sure that in some way she was going to be presented with some situation that would have her driving the team to move fast.

She smiled as she realized that Trey had detoured to her favorite store and said that he would go in and buy the bags of candy and that he only wanted to know how many bags to buy. She asked for at least a dozen bags, but she insisted that she pay.

She looked back at Johnnie and let him know that one was for him. She wanted him to scan the missing person reports for Hamilton County and every county that bordered it and gather all the ones about missing women. She asked him to keep an eye out for one that had happened in the last couple of days.

Johnnie nodded and said that he would do it, but he wondered if he could negotiate for a tray of her cookies instead of a bag of candy.

Alex smiled and nodded but stipulated that a tray of cookies would mean he would need to set up breakfast each morning for the two of them for the rest of the week.

Johnnie nodded and replied that was an easy ask.

She enjoyed their close relationship and thought of Johnnie as her second father. Johnnie was a few years older than her father. Older but she knew Johnnie was in great condition and was exceptionally strong. He had demonstrated his physical strength when he had lowered a reel of wire cable from the bed of a maintenance truck. He had backed her up when Trey had been in the hospital recovering from near death after being brutally beaten. He had demonstrated his strength by lowering a roll of wire cabling from the back of a maintenance truck and then his bravery by pulling the wire cable off that reel through the legs of the helicopter and tying it to a fire hydrant. When the copter went to take off to shoot at her it crashed to the ground as it tried to take off.

Trey returned with the bags of candy, and they drove on into Loveland.

They arrived at the police station where they were cordially greeted like a part of the Loveland unit.

Alex looked at Trey and commented that a few bags of candy went a long way in making friends.

Sheriff Williams greeted them, thanked Alex for the bag of chocolate, introduced his Friend Arthur Milster, Sheriff of Missteer and asked whether they were ready for lunch. He said that he preferred to have them listen to Sheriff Milster after lunch.

Alex handed Arthur a bag of chocolate candy and introduced Trey and Johnnie.

She then said that she was not sure that ready was the condition she would find herself in, but she was willing to have lunch first and then return to hear the details afterwards.

Johnnie spoke up and said that it sounded like a good plan. He wanted to enjoy the lunch and watch the Little Miami to see if there would be any logs floating downstream.

Alex smiled at the reference to logs floating downstream because this was a Johnnie euphemism for thinking deeply about a case. She knew that he was probably already figuring out how to get the information she had requested.

A short time later they arrived at the restaurant, and they sat at an outside table that indeed had a great view of the Little Miami. It had not rained for a few days, so the river was running calmly by. She figured no actual logs would be floating by.

Alex made sure that Johnnie had a view of the river. She was sure the only floating logs would be in Johnnie's mind.

Sheriff Williams volunteered to order for all of them, and everyone agreed to let him do it. He put in an order for three of his favorite tacos and made sure the waiter knew that he wanted one for each person. He also ordered one tostada for each person. The final order was for three orders of donut holes with chocolate and caramel sauce drizzled over them. He reassured Alex that donut holes would be more than enough for all of them.

Alex joked with him that he would need to let them sleep in his van after lunch to recover from all the food he had ordered.

He nodded and replied that he wasn't worried about any of them falling asleep when they listened to what Sheriff Milster shared with them.

Johnnie nodded and said that he already had a premonition of the story and he planned to enjoy lunch.

Alex agreed and added that she was especially looking forward to the dessert.

Sheriff Williams made sure that the conversation remained light. He asked each person to share a highlight about themselves.

He knew that his friend was feeling down and concerned about the fact that he had come up empty handed in trying to solve the cases of three missing women. His friend had worked for almost three years and had come up empty handed. All three cases were now cold, and they hung heavy on his friend's mind.

He knew how that felt because he had carried a similar weight for more than fifteen years when Annie, a young teenager, had gone missing, and the case went cold.

He also knew how he felt when Alex, against all odds, had solved the case and had rescued Annie and her two kids from the forests of Pennsylvania. Alex had become a person who he thought about often as he followed the cases, she took on that had stumped other agencies and then marveled when she solved them.

He was an ultimate Alex supporter.

Alex enjoyed the lunch, but she would have liked not to be anticipating some horrific case from Sheriff Milster.

After lunch they all rode back to the Loveland police station, to a conference room and sat around a large meeting table. Sheriff Williams had iced tea and lemonade brought in and when everyone was seated, he asked Sheriff Milster to share the situation he faced.

Alex asked Johnnie to connect his computer to the Cincinnati police computer and see if there would be anything like what Sheriff Milster was about to share.

Sheriff Milster said that he liked how fast Alex was planning to try to help. He added that he hoped she would be successful where he had failed.

Alex nodded and replied that she figured he had only bad news to share and that every case in the past that she had taken on had a sad or horrible beginning and she was only trying to be prepared.

Sheriff Milster then described having three missing persons reports about three young women that seemed to have no connection to each other. Each had occurred several years ago but almost exactly one month apart in his jurisdiction.

Each young lady was reported missing, but each had a very different disappearance scenario, and the three did not know each other. The only similarity was that each had gone out alone and had never returned.

He then described the first situation where the young lady had gone by herself to an outdoor concert and had never returned home. She was last seen by some of her friends talking to a young man that was described as dark haired and rather handsome. They had interviewed several additional people that had been at the concert but did not come up with anything.

The second young lady had gone out hiking along the country roads that were around her farm but never returned home. He had his men follow several hiking routes her mother described but again there was no additional evidence.

He had driven each potential road that the young woman might have hiked and had not seen anything.

The third had gone to a night club where she often went, and she was last seen leaving as she chatted with a person that one of the waitresses said was a slender dark haired rather good-looking guy. She had looked out the window as the two got into a black pickup truck.

When she was asked about a license plate number, she said that she had no clue, but she did comment about the license plate holder. She described it as bright silver with red devil horns on each corner. He had his men look for black trucks, but none had that type of license plate holder.

Alex felt a shiver go down her back. She asked if the sheriff had the names of the friends and of the waitress. She also asked if he knew the hiking path that the other young woman had taken.

He said that he had the names, but he had no knowledge of the exact hiking path that the young lady had taken. He had walked out to the first country road with that young lady's mother but even the mother was not sure which way she would have gone because there were several more crossroads that she may have chosen to go down.

He added that he had one of his units travel every road looking for any clues but after a week they had come up empty.

Alex nodded and added that it was most likely that she had been whisked away and was not to be found.

She looked at Johnnie and asked if he had any additional questions or information.

Johnnie nodded and said that he had only enough time to search Hamilton County and Warren County records. He said that he had two more counties in Ohio and then counties in Indiana and Kentucky to search. He said that so far, he had six additional missing person reports that met her search criteria. He speculated that the number could double.

Alex nodded and let everyone know that she would go back and see if her boss would let her take on the case. She added that it appeared to her that a serial killer was at work.

Sheriff Milster asked why she thought it was a serial killer.

She shook her head and said that it was just a premonition.

She then asked Johnnie to shut down his search, and they would go back to the office and once the case was officially agreed to, they would dig deeper and see if they could find who was doing the killing.

Both Sheriffs thanked her for coming out and listening to them and asked that they be contacted if the case was going to be taken up.

Alex said that she would of course do that. She then suggested that they give her Chief a call and request that he support making this an official case.

Sheriff Milster shook her hand and said that he was already feeling better and hoped that she would take on the case.

Once they were in the car Alex asked Johnnie how far back in time he had gone in his search.

Johnnie responded with the fact he had only searched back one year.

Alex asked him to do what he had done in the Pool of Blood case and determine when the serial killer had started his journey. She was not sure how long he had been at work but most likely his early years of his killing habit would have been at a low level.

Recent events may have triggered an increase in his activities. She asked Johnnie to identify the first victim and to chart out the hockey stick pattern she was expecting to see.

When they arrived at the station, Alex led the way to the Chief's office.

The Chief's door was open, and he waved her in. He asked whether he should call Bill and Trevor in.

Alex nodded and said that if he accepted the case she was about to describe, the case might cover the tri-state area and that would require a significant amount of coordination that would require their help.

The call from Loveland from the two sheriffs had prepared him and he had already alerted Bill and Trevor. He stepped to the door and signaled for them to come to his office.

Once everyone was in, he closed the door and asked Alex to fill them in on what she had learned over lunch with the two sheriffs. He shared the fact that both of them had talked to him and asked that he take up the case.

Alex positioned her chair so she could face the rest. She then took them through the details of the case and made the point that Johnnie had already surfaced six additional missing person reports that fit the description of the three missing person reports that Sheriff Milster had given them. She was relatively sure they were dealing with a serial killer who lived somewhere in the area and had recently increased his kill rate.

Bill asked why she thought the killing rate had gone up.

Alex replied that Johnnie had only gone back one year in his initial search and the number seemed high not to have been noticed earlier.

She had asked Johnnie to go back as far as possible to determine what the killing hockey stick data looked like. She commented that this was the approach that had helped her solve the case where she had dealt with a serial killer in Hawaii.

She added that she had promised Johnnie a tray of oatmeal raisin cookies for him to define the hockey stick for this case.

Trevor asked what he had to do to get a tray of her cookies.

Alex smiled and replied that Johnnie was checking the missing person reports in Hamilton County and all the surrounding counties and that they would need to interface with the seven counties that surrounded Cincinnati. She would like him and Bill to be the face of the team to each of the organizations involved and get them to give the team legal access to their missing persons reports.

Trevor gave a groan and asked why Johnnie got the easy work and he and Bill got the hard stuff.

Alex smiled and said that to make the deal a little sweeter she would add a tray of brownies to the deal. She added that this case gave him a chance to be in the news and she was doing this because she wanted to flaunt his superior capabilities.

Bill smiled and added that he knew that it was because, "she loved them too."

Alex smiled and said that the only person not getting any cookies promised to him was Trey, but she planned to bring a batch over to his house as soon as she received his next invitation to a back yard cook out.

The Chief spoke up and said that he was officially launching the investigation into a potential serial killer, and he would let the hierarchy know. He wanted it all kept low key until they were close to capturing the killer.

He did not want the news speculating on a potential serial killer operating in the Cincinnati area.

Alex said that she agreed to keep it low key and that the only other person in the department that she wanted to read in was Dr. Rogers. She figured his help would be critical if they found any bodies.

The Chief called the meeting to an end and suggested that the five of them figure out how to attack the case.

Alex led the way out of the office. She suggested that they spend the rest of the afternoon outlining how they would handle the case and what each of them would do. Then they could reconvene in the morning and set up a detailed plan.

Johnnie said that would give him some time to decide how to best reapply his Hawaii data search technique. He shared that he had learned a ton about programing in both the legal side and on the hacking side since then and thought he might be able to speed up the search.

Alex said that she was counting on him being able to give the team a way to identify this mysterious young man who drove a black pickup with red horns on the rear license plate holder.

Thanks for reading this far; To finish the previewed to story go to:

https://www.remwriter95.net/

About the Author

Ronald E. Mueller
remwriter95@gmail.com

Ron grew up in what is now Flint River State Park in Southeast Iowa. The 170-year-old house Ron lived in is built into a hillside. It faces a 125-foot-high cliff towering over the little Flint River. The house and the land talked to him about; the passing of time, the struggle to conquer the land, the struggles people faced and the wonder of nature.

He climbed the cliffs, crawled into the caves, dove from the swimming rock, collected clams from the bottom of the pond, gigged and skinned frogs for their legs. He trapped muskrats for fur, hunted raccoon in the dead of night, and with only a stick hunted rabbits in the dead of winter.

His young life was outdoors, and nature tested him.

He walked to a one room stone schoolhouse uphill both ways. A stern but warm-hearted teacher, Mrs. Henry was instrumental in shaping his character as she shepherded him from the fourth to the eighth grade.

It was a great way to grow up.

Ron graduated from Burlington, High School, went to Vietnam in the Navy. He graduated from The University of South Florida with a master's degree in engineering, worked for thirty eight years for Procter and Gamble, traveled around the world thirty times.

He has remained happily married for more than fifty years. His daughter and his two sons are all successful and his three grandchildren have all graduated.

His wife has humored and supported him as he became a full time professional story teller.

He has come to realize that he is, what is known as, a Cozy writer. Excitement and adventure but little guts and gore. His heroine or hero suffer a little but live happily ever after.

His experiences inter-twined with snippets of fantasy lend themselves to the adventures he leads the reader through.

His experiences inter-twined with snippets of fantasy lend themselves to the adventures he leads the reader through.

Books by the Author

Fiction Series
The Alex Evercrest Series
The River Front
The Girl on The Grill
Missing
Maggot
Racist
Votive Candles
Windy City
Country Road
Pool of Blood
Sins of the Daughter
Body Parts
The Skull Collector
The Vanishing
The Shadow Fighter
Moonshine
Grief's Trajectory
The Magic Touch
Northern Lights
Alex Evercrest Heroine
Alex Evercrest Collection Two
New Direction
A Family Affair
Disruption
The St. Lebuinnus Church Murder

A Brian O'Neil Novel
Hawaiian Phoenix
Moon Curser
Death Broker

The Problem Solver Series
Solutions
Drug Lords
Border Crosser
The Problem Solver Collection

The Taelo Series
Taelo: The Early Years
Taelo: The Golden Feather
Taelo: Journey of Discovery
Taelo: Dangerous Passage
Taelo: Condor Clan Slingers
Taelo: Circumvention
Taelo: The Journey of Sages
Taelo: Collection
Taelo: Future Leaders Journey
A Taelo Story:
White Swan and Quiet Pheasant
The Child's Name
Floating Cloud
Quiet Rabbit
Busy Bee

Little Otter & Talking Wren
Broken Spear
Burley Bear & Meadow Flower
Taelo Story Collection

<u>Science Fiction</u>

The Savitar Series
Journey's End
Savitar
Confluence
Savitar Series Collection

The Door Series
The Door
Aliens We
The Endless Hole
The Swarm
Esoteric Journey
The Gentle Eye
The Door Series Collection

Bram Nielson Series
The Fold
The Message
Fold Wormhole
Negative Fold
Ripples in Time
Bram Nielson Collection

<u>Single Science Fiction Books:</u>
Current Past and Future
The Event
The Door
Viajante 7

Characters in the Story

Alex	Cathy	Evercrest	Police Detective Main Character
Matthew	Timothy	Knolton	Alex's suitor
Rose-Anne	Germain	Evercrest	Alex's mother
Russel	Johnson	Evercrest	Alex's father
Helping Hands charity			Alex's nonprofit org
Trey		McGregor	Alex's Detective Partner
Lindsey		McGregor	Wife
Nolan		McGregor	Son
Johnnie		Smith	Old Viet Vet
Mary		Higgins	Johnnie's Phili "friend"
Bruce	Lincoln	Johnson	Cin Chief of Detectives
Mary-Anne	Leslie	Johnson	Chiefs Wife
Bill	Hamilton	Danson	Detective
Travis	Bailey	Carter	Detective
Dr. Rogers			Coroner
Jane	Elousie	Stradford	Lieutenant Governor
Felix			proprietor of the fishing dock
Golden Goose			Name of the Yacht
Sandra		Olson	Policewoman guard
Annie	Lorie	Scots	Missing girl
Linda		Annies	older daughter
Lorie		Annies	second daughter
Harold		Zimmerman	Chicago DEA
James	Oscor	Kaizer	Sheriff of Wiggin
Abbie	Alisa	Bender	protect Alex married James
John	S.	Williams	Lawyer that was abused
Hanna		Waverly	John's mate
Angelica			Angel on the hill
Brian		Lexter	Cincinnati FBI Bureau Chief
Cais		Leu	Alex's Viet friend
Tracy		Hunter	Trey's Analyst

https://www.remwriter95.net/

Published by: Around the World Publishing LLC.